The KenKen Killings

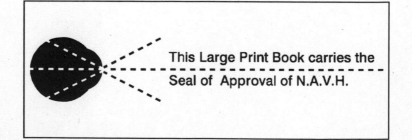

This Large Print Book carries the
Seal of Approval of N.A.V.H.

A PUZZLE LADY MYSTERY

The KenKen Killings

Parnell Hall

THORNDIKE PRESS

A part of Gale, Cengage Learning

GALE
CENGAGE Learning·

Detroit • New York • San Francisco • New Haven, Conn • Waterville, Maine • London

GALE
CENGAGE Learning

LIBRARY OF CONGRESS CATALOGING-IN-PUBLICATION DATA

Hall, Parnell.
  The kenken killings : a puzzle lady mystery / by Parnell Hall.
     p. cm. — (Thorndike Press large print mystery)
  ISBN-13: 978-1-4104-3743-3 (hardcover)
  ISBN-10: 1-4104-3743-4 (hardcover)
  1. Felton, Cora (Fictitious character)—Fiction. 2.
Puzzles—Fiction. 3. Murder—Investigation—Fiction. 4. Large
type books. I. Title.
PS3558.A37327K46 2011b
813'.54—dc22   2011003365

Published in 2011 by arrangement with St. Martin's Press, LLC.

L-T-M

Printed in the United States of America
1 2 3 4 5 6 7 15 14 13 12 11

For Dennis,
who stayed home

KENKEN KUDOS

I would like to thank Tetsuya Miyamoto, for inventing KenKen® as a means to help his students learn math; Will Shortz, for popularizing this wonderful creation by featuring it in *The New York Times,* as well as in his series of bestselling books; and Robert Fuhrer, president of Nextoy, LLC, of which KenKen® is a registered trademark, for granting the permissions and supplying the puzzles that appear in this book.

I would like to thank Manny Nosowsky, for creating the crossword puzzles. Manny is invaluable. I couldn't kill people without him.

Last but not least, I would like to thank Ellen Ripstein, for editing the puzzles and catching my mistakes.

Without these people, this book would not have been possible.

CHAPTER 1

Cora Felton jumped in the air and clicked her heels together, a perilous undertaking since she was wearing high heels and had put on a little weight.

"Good Lord! What is it?" Sherry Carter said.

"Chester T. Markowitz is dead."

"Who?"

"My husband."

"Your husband?"

"Yes."

"You have a husband named Chester T. Markowitz?"

"Not anymore."

"But you did?"

"Apparently."

Sherry sighed. Her aunt's loopy behavior could be frustrating at times, and this was one of them. "I give up. I assume you'll tell me about it when you're good and ready."

"I'll tell you about it when I know myself,"

Cora said. "But I'm as much at sea as you are."

"Oh, for goodness' sakes. Do you or do you not have a dead husband?"

"I have several." Cora shrugged. "As to this one, I really couldn't say."

Sherry grabbed the letter out of Cora's hand, looked it over. Her eyes widened. "According to this, you not only have a dead husband, he seems to have left you a bit of money."

Cora beamed. "Yes. Isn't that nice?"

"Not if it's a mistake. Not if the money is supposed to go to someone else."

"Who?" Cora said. "If some scheming hussy got her claws on poor Chester —"

Sherry cut her off. "Can we go outside? You're making a scene."

Sherry and Cora were in the Bakerhaven Post Office. Like most town residents, they got their mail delivered. This morning there was a notice in the box saying that Cora had a registered letter. That did not bode well. Usually registered letters meant lawsuits, unpaid bills, late tax returns, and the like.

Cora Felton had all the business acumen of a hyperactive Labradoodle puppy, and Sherry was used to rescuing her from one financial crisis after another.

10

Sherry wrestled her aunt outside, looked around to see that no one was within earshot. "Okay. Now you can talk without fear of making the *National Enquirer.* Who the hell is Chester T. Markowitz?"

Cora smiled, the trademark Puzzle Lady smile that graced the crossword puzzle column that Sherry wrote for her. Cora couldn't construct a crossword puzzle with a gun to her head. Her niece was the real cruciverbalist. When Sherry created the column, she used her aunt's image to hide from her abusive ex-husband. It hadn't occurred to her that the Puzzle Lady would become nationally famous, do breakfast cereal commercials, and be stuck with the pretense forever.

"It's simple," Cora said. "Since I quit drinking, there are parts of my life I can't remember. The eighties, for instance. It's entirely possible I married this gentleman, though I can't recall him at all."

"But . . ."

"But what?"

"You had other husbands. You were married and divorced. Several times."

"What's your point?"

"If Mr. Markowitz was living, those marriages weren't legal."

"So?"

11

"You collected alimony. You inherited from some of them."

"Oh, I doubt if they'd mind. Particularly the dead ones. Anyway, what's the big deal? Some lawyer says I've got some money coming. You think I'm not going to take it?"

"I'm sure you are. It's just something we should do without a brass band. From a public relations angle."

"Oh, who could possibly care?"

"The kids who eat breakfast cereal. More to the point, the *parents* of the kids who eat breakfast cereal. If Granville Grains finds out they hired a bigamous spokesperson, they're not going to be happy."

"Oh, you're just an old worrywart. I came into an inheritance. Let's stop by the candy store, pick up some chocolates."

"You sound just like a kid."

"I feel like a kid," Cora said. "Yesterday I was a spinster aunt." She smiled. "Today I'm a widow!"

CHAPTER 2

"I can't believe you bought so much chocolate," Sherry said.

"It's a special occasion."

"It's always a special occasion. The sun rising is a special occasion."

"So what?"

"You're putting on a little weight."

"You should talk."

Sherry flushed. Sherry was a newlywed, and ever since she got home from the honeymoon, her aunt had teased her about getting pregnant. So she'd put on some water weight lately. That didn't mean anything. Not necessarily. But Sherry had a hard time denying it, particularly since she and Aaron had begun construction on an addition to the modest ranch house she shared with her aunt.

As Cora turned into the driveway, a backhoe was wreaking havoc in the side lawn.

"How am I supposed to get any work

done with that racket?" Cora said.

"What work?"

"My crossword puzzle column."

"I write your crossword puzzle column."

"Exactly."

Sherry got out of the car.

The contractor came up to meet them. Cora knew he was the contractor because he wore a suit and had a blueprint.

"Mrs. Grant . . . ," he said.

"Mrs. Grant? Good Lord. Are you Mrs. Grant?"

"I got married, Cora."

"Right. You're Mrs. Grant, and I'm the widow Markowitz. I must keep these things straight."

"Is there a problem?" Sherry asked.

"A little. We hit bedrock. We can't dig it. We'll have to blast."

"You're going to dynamite our house?" Cora said.

"Not your house. Just your lawn."

"You will tell us when. So I can keep the dog in."

"You'll probably want to stay somewhere else during the demolition."

"So you *are* going to blast the house."

"We're not blasting the house. But if a stray rock —"

"A stray rock? Tell me you're not talking

14

about a stray rock."

"Cora, let me talk to Mr. Fisher."

"Be my guest."

Cora opened the door and let the dog out. Buddy shot from the house, barking, spinning, and marking his territory. He was peeing on the backhoe as she went inside.

Cora clattered down the hallway to her bedroom, kicked off her dress shoes. She had put them on because of the registered letter. Which was silly. The writer of the letter wouldn't see the person who picked it up. But registered letters meant trouble. If she was marched off to jail, Cora wanted to look her best. Even if she wasn't marched off to jail yet but merely informed such an outcome was in the offing.

Well, what a happy development. In a matter of minutes she had gone from a felon in heels to a widow in flats.

Cora went back in the office, sat at the computer, Googled "Chester T. Markowitz." He didn't Google. That was strange. Everybody Googled. But Chester T. Markowitz had not one single hit.

She left out the *t,* Googled "Chester Markowitz." That was worse. Now she had fifty thousand hits.

Sherry came into the office. "What are you doing?"

"Googling Chester T. Markowitz."

"Any luck?"

"There's a million Chesters, and no Chester T.'s."

"Get up."

Sherry sat at the computer. Her fingers flew over the keyboard. Images jumped across the screen. Pages opened and closed in the wink of an eye.

Sherry pushed back from the desk, turned to Cora. "All right. I don't know anything about Chester. But the lawyer is a shyster."

"The lawyer?"

"Well, that's who you're dealing with. Mr. Markowitz is dead."

"I don't see why you're making such a big deal out of this. If the guy wants to give me money, why can't I take it?"

"You gotta make sure it's not bogus. Like those Internet scams."

"What Internet scams?"

"Like the spam you get. You know, 'I'm a Nairobian prince being deprived of my sixty-two-million-dollar inheritance, which I can't collect because I don't have the ten thousand dollars to buy my way out of servitude and come to America.' "

"You mean Sambora wasn't real? I was wondering why he didn't write."

"Cora. You didn't."

"No, I didn't. You're a total killjoy. Are you going to let me have my ten grand or not?"

"The ten grand for the Nairobian prince?"

"No, the ten grand from Chester T. Markowitz. According to the lawyer, all I have to do is send the confirmation of my address and he'll send me a check."

"There's gotta be a catch to it."

"Why?"

"It's too easy."

"Come on, Sherry. We need the money."

"We don't need the money."

"I thought we were building a house."

"It's financed."

"Financing doesn't solve anything. It's like digging a hole and burying your future in it."

"Who told you that?"

"Some husband or other. I forget. Anyway, you're building a house and I'd like to contribute."

"You're contributing. You know how much your sudoku books are bringing in?"

"I know they're doing well."

"Yes, they are. So are your crossword puzzle books. Of course, I have to write them."

"How did you change the subject?"

"What subject?"

"Ten grand. Chester T. Markowitz."

"Cora. It's a scam. Like the Nairobian prince."

"It's *not* like the Nairobian prince. He's not *asking* me for ten thousand dollars. He's *giving* me ten thousand dollars. How can there be a catch?"

"Cora —"

"According to this letter, all I have to do is confirm my address and I get a check for ten grand. What's the downside?"

"Receiving money under false pretenses."

"What's false about it?"

"You don't know Chester T. Markowitz."

"Come on, Sherry. No one's asking me if I knew the guy, or was married to the guy, or even heard of the guy. All they're asking me to do is confirm my address. I've never *denied* my address." Cora glanced out the window. "Unless the addition alters the address. Do we have to put a half after the street number?"

"I don't like it."

Cora patted her niece on the cheek. "Sherry. Sweetie. How could it possibly hurt?"

CHAPTER 3

Lennie Fleckstein's eyes popped open. Was that light peeking through the window? It was, wasn't it. His wife always pulled the blinds closed, and the light always seeped through. Blackout shades, that's what he needed. Not likely, it would ruin the decor, such as it was. He was stuck with blinds that let in light at the first crack of dawn.

What time was it, anyway?

Lennie squinted at the digital readout on the TV. *Eight* o'clock? How the hell did it get to be *eight* o'clock? Eight o'clock wasn't dawn, eight o'clock was eight o'clock. The blinds were *selectively* letting in light, waking him when they damn well felt like it.

Lennie tossed off the covers.

Emma turned, flailed, snarled, "What are you doing?"

"Getting up."

"Now?"

"It's eight o'clock."

"That late? What did you do, close the blinds?"

"I'm getting up."

"You're always going to oversleep if you close the blinds."

Emma rolled over and went back to sleep.

Lennie sighed, clambered out of bed. What the hell difference did it make if he didn't wake up until eight. He didn't get to the office until ten, sometimes later. Not that it mattered. Not that anyone cared. Not like he had a partner who would be sitting there tapping his watch. Lennie knew what he had to do and when he had to do it. His practice paid for the office and the house and the car and the TV and the goddamned bed she was sleeping in, for chrissake. So who was she to tell him when to get up?

Not that he would ever say so, because that would be rude and uncaring, and Emma might need a lawyer, might have already met one, a tricky scheming shyster who might interpret that remark as a reason why Emma should be entitled to the house and the car and the TV and at least fifty percent of anything Lennie might earn for the rest of his natural life. That was without the mental cruelty angle, and with any lawyer worth his salt there was sure to be mental cruelty involved. Though Lennie knew in his heart of hearts, but would not be able to demonstrate it on the stand, that if anyone was guilty of mental cruelty in the marriage, it was undoubtedly her.

Lennie thought all that as he shuffled into the kitchen to make a cup of coffee. He did it every day. Made a cup of coffee. And thought all that.

Lennie took his cup of coffee out in the driveway and started up the Mercedes. It was an old Mercedes, but it still counted as a gas-guzzling status symbol. Lennie held the coffee cup in one hand, backed insolently down the driveway with the other. He veered out onto the drive, slammed on the brake for a speeding Prius, and called on the gods of procreation as well as the gods of other pagan rituals less likely to result in progeny.

Lennie set the cup on but not in the cup holder, which was not designed for a cup with a handle, and pulled into traffic. He considered running the Prius off the road just for spite. Decided against it. His insurance premiums were already through the roof.

Lennie parked his car as usual in the Walgreens parking lot, trotted upstairs, and opened his office.

The answering machine was not beeping.

That was good in that no one wanted to sue him, bad in that there was no work.

Lennie sat at the desk, clicked the mouse on the computer. He left it running all night since the computer nerd who fixed it told him it cost as much energy to restart as it did to just run. Lennie wasn't sure if the guy was kidding, but in Lennie's book, inaction beat action every time.

Lennie opened up his e-mail. Six new messages came through. Four were spam. One was an online bill.

The sixth was from puzzlelady.com.

Could that be who he thought it was?

Lennie clicked the mouse, opened the e-mail.

Hot damn!

Lennie snatched up the phone, made the call.

"Hello?"

"It's me."

"So?"

"She took it!"

CHAPTER 4

Sherry Carter came out of the kitchen with plates of food piled high. "Here we go."

Cora looked at it. "Salmon, broccoli, and rice. Seems aggressively healthy."

"You like salmon."

"I do. I just noticed you've been cooking more nutritious meals of late. As if it were important."

"It is important."

"Uh-huh," Cora said. "Since you got off on this health kick, I've dropped five pounds. How much have you lost?"

"I haven't weighed myself."

"You probably should. You don't want to become anorexic."

"I'm not anorexic."

"I'll say. You look nice and fat and goosey. Isn't there some song like that, Aaron? About nice and fat and goosey. Keeping your women that way."

"As I recall, it's fat and *drunk* and goosey,"

Sherry said.

"Oh, low blow!" Cora said. "I must have struck a nerve. It's not like you to lash out like that."

"What? Quoting a song lyric? You brought it up."

"Even so." Cora turned to Aaron. "You been noticing these mood swings lately?"

"I do not have mood swings!" Sherry protested.

"See?" Cora said. "Like that."

"Aaron, defend me from this woman."

"My wife does not have mood swings."

"Wow! That's pretty persuasive. I don't know how I can argue with that. Did you know your husband was so good at debate when you married him, or is this an added perk?" Cora took a bite of salmon, chewed it around. "You know, for healthy food this is awfully damn good."

"Delicious," Aaron said.

"Oh. Bad line reading," Cora said. "Way too automatic and mechanical. You'd think this was your fifth child."

Sherry slammed down a fork. "Oh, for God's sake! When we decide to have children, *we'll* tell *you*."

"That's very considerate of you, since I tried to move out and you guilted me into staying."

24

"You got a letter," Sherry said, bluntly changing the subject.

"What do you mean?"

"The postman came, put a letter in the box. I came home, took a letter out of the box. Isn't that how it works?"

"Where is it?"

"Kitchen table."

"Why didn't you give it to me?"

"You didn't go in the kitchen."

Cora sighed, lifted the plate off her lap, put it on the coffee table.

"I'll get it," Aaron said.

He hopped up, went and fetched the letter.

"Well, what is it?"

"I don't know. Some law firm in Great Neck. Here."

Cora's eyes lit up. "Really?" She tore open the envelope, pulled out a check. "Hallelujah!" She pointed her finger at Sherry. "In your face, doubting Thomas! This will tide me over till my next book."

"What is it?" Aaron said.

"My inheritance. From the late, lamented Chester T. Markowitz. Your little wife here thought it was a scam."

"Is that a real check?" Sherry said skeptically.

"Of course it's a real check."

"From Chester T. Markowitz?"

"Don't be silly. Dead men don't send checks. It's from the law firm of Fleckstein and Stone, conservator for the estate of Chester T. Markowitz."

"Signed by the attorney?"

"Well, it's not signed by Chester."

"And it's made out to you?"

Cora blinked. "Yes, it's made out to me."

"You hesitated."

"No, I didn't."

Sherry smiled. "Cora, I've watched you interrogate suspects. You just exhibited all the classic signs you look for. Didn't she, Aaron?"

Aaron looked at Sherry. At Cora. Back at Sherry.

Cora grinned. "Oh ho, you put *him* on the spot! He doesn't dare cross you in your condition —"

"In my *condition?*" Sherry caught herself. "Nice try. Don't change the subject. You hesitated when I asked if the check was made out to you. Why does that make you uneasy?"

"Boy, you'd have made a demon prosecutor. I'd watch out, Aaron. You're in as much trouble as if you'd married Becky Baldwin."

Even mention of the attractive attorney who was Aaron's ex-girlfriend couldn't sidetrack Sherry. If anything, it made her more suspicious. "What's wrong with the check?"

"There's nothing 'wrong' with it. It's made out to Cora Felton Markowitz."

"Oh, for goodness' sakes!"

"Well, why wouldn't it be, if I'm the widow? What's the difference?"

"You know the difference. You can sign a check made out to Cora Felton and you haven't committed a crime. You haven't obtained money under false pretenses, forged a document, and perpetrated a fraud on the court."

"Court? What court?"

"I don't know. I'm not a lawyer."

"Maybe you should have married Becky," Cora said. "Well, if you kids are gonna argue . . ."

"Sit down!" Sherry took a breath. "Look, Cora, you're a brilliant woman. At solving crimes you have no equal. If this check were made out to any other person whatsoever, you'd be the first to point out all the reasons they shouldn't sign it. But wave ten grand in your face —"

"Ten grand!" Aaron said.

Sherry threw up her hands. "Oh, for goodness' sakes. Yes, Aaron. Ten grand. This check is worth ten grand."

"Which is why I'm not leaping to embrace the suggestion that I treat it like scrap paper," Cora said.

Aaron frowned. "Anything else on the check?"

"No. Just the notation."

"What notation?"

"Widow's inheritance."

"Oh?"

"Which doesn't mean anything. Anyone can write anything on a check. All I've gotta do is take it down to the bank and cash it."

"As the widow Markowitz."

"As Cora Felton. I'll deposit it to my account. The account of Cora Felton."

"And you'll sign it on the back?"

"Yes, I'll sign it on the back." Cora turned the check over, uttered a brief, terse comment that had little to do with banking.

"What's the matter?" Sherry said.

"It's nothing."

"And it didn't bother you. Yes, I noticed. Just what is this nothing that didn't bother you?"

"It's a lawyer's check. He typed a release."

"No kidding. What's it say?"

Cora took a breath. She read, " 'I, Cora Felton Markowitz, do hereby agree that the amount of this check, to wit ten thousand dollars, represents the entire amount of the

28

inheritance specified and/or implied in the last will and testament of my husband, Chester T. Markowitz, and I hereby relinquish any and all claims on any and all moneys which might be discovered to be part of the estate of the said Chester T. Markowitz.' "

"Gee," Sherry said. "*That's* not a red flag."

"Oh, come on. What could possibly go wrong?"

CHAPTER 5

Chief Dale Harper parked the police car at the top of the driveway, got out, and surveyed the new addition. It was nearly finished. The backhoe was long gone, and the crew was down to a carpenter and a painter, mostly working on the trim.

Cora came walking up. "Like it?"

"That comply with local zoning ordinances?"

"Be a hell of a time to find out it didn't."

"Are you allowed in?"

"Don't wanna upset the contractor. Until he's done, it's his house. If I poke my nose in, I'm delaying some painter or other and adding five hundred bucks to the job. It's the reason I never had a maid. I wouldn't be allowed in the house." Cora frowned. "As I recall, Henry hired one. Just before the divorce."

"Suppose you were allowed in the house. What would you find?"

"Aha!" Cora pointed to the second floor. "Bedroom, master bath. Two small bedrooms with bath."

"Each?"

"No. One for the two. A hardship, but you gotta make sacrifices."

"The master bedroom is yours?"

"Yeah, right. That was the original plan, but that was a month ago. Now I doubt if I'm allowed upstairs."

"Oh?"

"I think they're starting a family. Sherry says no, but that doesn't stop me from kidding her. Anyway, they're moving upstairs. I'm left with the house. Except for the office. And the kitchen. And the living room. I think I get to keep my bedroom, but I'm not sure. Actually, there's a perfectly nice living room over there. Along with what Sherry refers to as a 'modern kitchen.' Which I'm sure is also perfectly nice, but with the assessment of 'modern' hanging over its head, I doubt it will be used much."

"Are you allowed in the living room?"

"In theory. It would have been so much easier for them just to throw me out."

"There's a basement?"

"There is indeed. After living on a slab all these years, it's a thing of beauty and a joy forever. Of course, it's a problem."

"Why?"

"Well, there's a furnace room and a laundry room and a half bath. And a storage closet and a freezer chest. Can't argue with that. The rest of the basement's the bone of contention."

"How come?"

"I want a pool table." Cora frowned. "Don't look at me like that. As a girl, I was good. Used to hustle beers playing bar pool."

"Sherry said no?"

"Sherry said yes."

"What's the problem?"

"Sherry also said she's not knocked up."

"That's a nice way to put it."

"It is, isn't it? I was going to say a bun in the oven, but it seemed too wordy. Anyway, the pool room is now a game room."

"So, your idea of a game room . . ."

"Is pool, poker, and penny ante bridge. The three p's. Not tricycles and building blocks."

"Cora, even if that were true, it's years away. Kids are small. They don't get around much."

"I know."

"So what's the problem?"

Cora made a face. "They won't let me smoke."

"What?"

"They say I can't smoke in the addition."

"Well, it's nice and new there, why should it smell like an ashtray?"

"Because I'm in it."

Harper smiled. "I see your problem."

"So?"

"You may have to quit smoking."

"You're a big help. You know what it took me to quit drinking?"

Harper started to answer, flushed. It had taken a man to make her stop drinking. The chief didn't want to point that out. It was a rhetorical question, anyway. Cora was in full grumbling mode, and nothing was going to make a difference.

"Listen. The reason I dropped by . . ,"

"It wasn't just to see the house?"

"No. I got a crime scene."

"Someone's dead?"

"No one's dead. There's other crimes besides murder. And other crime scenes. This one's a robbery."

"Well, that's something. What was taken?"

"Nothing."

Cora scowled. "Chief, are you messing with me? Believe me, I'm not in the mood."

"I can see that." As she started to flare up, he quickly added, "Roger Randolph. You know him? The banker."

"He owns a bank?"

"He works in it. Not as a teller, but at a desk. He approves loans."

"He doesn't turn them down?" Cora said dryly.

"You get turned down for a loan?"

"I haven't tried to get one. I just have a thing with job titles. 'He approves loans.' It means he also rejects them. But you don't hear a guy introduced as 'He rejects loans.' The guy evaluates and decides on loan applications. Isn't that what he does?"

"Yes."

"To say he approves them makes him sound like such a good fellow."

"Well, whatever you want to call him, he got home from the bank this afternoon and found he'd been robbed."

"Of nothing." Cora nodded. "It was probably someone who asked for a loan and *got* nothing. You're bringing me a nonexistent crime. A robbery that didn't happen. Too bad it wasn't a murder. We could interview the corpse."

"Would you be happier with the term *attempted robbery?*"

"I don't know. What did the robber attempt to steal?"

Harper frowned. "That's the problem."

"Nothing? The robber attempted to steal

nothing? And the robber *succeeded* in stealing nothing. That's not an attempted robbery. That's a fait accompli."

"Anyway, Randolph's mighty upset about it."

"A robbery that didn't happen? Yeah, that would upset me."

"The perpetrator got into his house, went upstairs, lifted down the picture over his bed, and opened the wall safe."

"But they didn't take anything?"

"No."

"Why not?"

"There was nothing in the safe."

"So, what's the problem?"

"There is now."

CHAPTER 6

Roger Randolph lived at the top of the hill in a two-story frame house, white with black trim, like the majority of houses in Baker-haven. The banker, a slight man with a milquetoast complexion, met them outside. His manner was much more ingratiating than Cora imagined it must be when approving loans.

"I'm glad you're taking this seriously," he said. "Considering nothing was stolen."

"It's still an unlawful entry," Harper said. "That's serious."

"Assuming you didn't leave the door unlocked," Cora said.

Randolph frowned, immediately looked much more the way Cora had envisioned him.

"I assume you know Cora Felton?"

"Only by reputation. I've seen you around town."

"You make me sound like a lady of the evening."

Randolph blushed.

"I'm kidding. Come on, let's see your safe."

The banker led them upstairs to the bedroom. The picture lay on the bed. The safe was open.

"This is just the way you found it?" Cora said.

"That's right."

"And why did you leave it this way?"

He pointed at Chief Harper. "He told me to."

"I wanted you to see it," Harper said.

"How come?"

"Because there's something in the safe."

"If it's a crossword puzzle, I'll kill you."

"It isn't."

Cora reached in, pulled out a sheet of paper.

4×		7+	
	12×	2÷	3−
1−			
	1	1−	

Her eyes widened. "Oh, my God. It's a Ken-Ken®."

"What's that?"

"The new number puzzle. Haven't you seen them? They have them every day in *The New York Times*."

Harper flushed slightly. Cora realized he didn't read it.

"What does it mean?" he asked.

"Nothing. It's just numbers."

"It's not just numbers." Harper pointed. "There are pluses and minuses."

"Operations. Addition, subtraction, multiplication, and division. All the numbers in a darkly outlined area will add, subtract, multiply, or divide to yield the number by the operation sign."

"You lost me."

"Oh, come on. It's easy. Look at the last two boxes in the first row across. See the number 7+? That means the numbers in those two boxes add up to 7. So they could only be 3 and 4."

"Or 5 and 2," Harper pointed out.

Cora shook her head. "Couldn't be. This is a 4-by-4 KenKen. It uses only the numbers 1, 2, 3, 4. Each number appears once, and only once, in every row or column. It's like sudoku with math."

"I see," Harper said.

Cora had a feeling he was just saying that. "Of course you do. So the only two numbers that give you 7+ have to be 3 and 4. Or 4 and 3. They could be in either order. But only one is right."

"How do you know which?"

"They have to fit in with the other rows and columns. 7+ tells you the answer will be 3 and 4 or 4 and 3. You have to narrow it down."

"How?"

"Okay. Look just below those two boxes. See the 3- in the second box down in the last vertical column? That means one of the two numbers in the darkly outlined boxes will subtract from the other to make 3. The only two numbers that do that are 4 and 1."

"Which is which?"

"You don't know that yet. But one of those boxes is a 4, and one of them is a 1. That means the box directly above the 3- can't be a 4. Because there can't be two 4's in that column."

"So?"

"That tells you where your 3 and 4 go in your 7+ boxes. The last box can't be a 4, so it has to be a 3. So the other box, the one with the little 7+ in it, has to be a 4."

"Uh-huh. What else can you tell?"

"See the box on the bottom of the second column? With the dark line all around it and the 1 in the corner?"

"Yeah."

"That's a gift. You don't have to do anything. That tells you that box is a 1."

"I like that."

"I thought you would. And the two boxes with the 12× have to be 3 and 4, because they multiply to give you 12. And do you know what that means?"

"No, but I'm sure you're going to tell me."

"That means the square just above them, the top square in the second column down, has to be a 2."

"Why?"

"Because you already have a 1, 3, and 4 in the column, and the column has to have one of each number."

"Yeah," Harper said. "But now look. That 4× in the upper left corner has *three* squares marked off together."

"Right. It's a triple. That means the three numbers multiply to make 4. The only three numbers that do that are 2, 2, and 1."

"That's not true," Roger Randolph said. "What about 4, 1, and 1?"

"Ah, the banker chimes in," Cora said. "Yes, 4, 1, and 1 do multiply and give you 4. But it can't be that in this case, because we just filled in the top square in the second column with a 2. That's one of our three numbers. So it has to be 2, 2, and 1."

"I thought you couldn't have two 2's," Chief Harper said.

"You can as long as they're not in the same row or column. Which is great. It tells you where they go. The 2's have to be on the wings of the triple, and the 1 has to be in between them in the square with the 4×."

"I'll take your word for it," Harper said. "Just solve the damn thing."

"Mind if I write on this?"

"Not at all."

Cora solved the KenKen.

1	2	4	3
2	3	1	4
3	4	2	1
4	1	3	2

"So, what does it mean?"

"It doesn't mean anything."

"But it has to."

"Why?"

"It was left there."

"So?"

"Someone went to a lot of trouble to break in here and leave it."

"Yes, they did."

"Why?"

"I have no idea."

"Aren't you curious?"

"Yes, I am. If you find out, I'd like to know."

"You're not going to help me solve this?"

"Solve what? The crime that wasn't?"

"Someone clearly wants you to."

"Why do you say that?"

"Because of the number puzzle."

"It's a KenKen."

"Whatever. The fact is you're being challenged."

"I'm always being challenged. It's like open season on the Puzzle Lady around here."

"You're not going to do anything?"

"There's nothing to do. This either means nothing, in which case there's nothing we have to do. Or it means something we don't know, so there's nothing we *can* do."

That answer did not satisfy Roger Randolph. "So, what *are* you going to do?" he said irritably.

Cora frowned. "It's Thursday, isn't it?"

"Yeah. So?"

She smiled. "I'm going to play bridge."

CHAPTER 7

"Four hearts," Cora said.

Iris Cooper's face fell. The first selectman had just bid three no-trump and was obviously looking forward to playing a cold contract. Iris was not at all happy to have her partner take her out.

Cora wasn't sorry. With a singleton ace of spades and no other outside entry, she was happy to play in hearts.

Cora smiled when she saw the dummy. Iris had a king, queen, doubleton of hearts. Cora didn't have the ace. In no-trump, the defenders could have knocked out her only entry, rendering the long suit worthless. Iris, trying to take nine tricks without it, would have fallen one short.

"I lose a heart and a club, making five," Cora said, tabling her hand.

Iris Cooper looked at the cards and smiled. "Oh. I see. Well done."

"This round's on me," Cora said. She

44

looked around for a waiter.

Cora was playing penny-a-point bridge in the bar of the Country Kitchen, Baker-haven's popular home-style restaurant. The bridge group played there every Thursday night. Cora had joined the game when she was still drinking. Somehow the transition hadn't bothered her.

Cora caught the waiter's eye. "I'm having a Diet Coke with a twist of lemon. These bad girls are drinking booze. Fill 'em up, and put it on my tab."

The waiter was just leaving when a middle-aged man in a business suit said, "Are you the Puzzle Lady?"

Cora didn't like being approached by fans, particularly when she was playing bridge. But the man wasn't bad-looking, and pick-ings had been slim. She mustered a smile. "That's me."

"Miss Cora Felton, the Puzzle Lady?"

"That's right. I'm playing cards right now, but if you'd care to stick around . . ."

"That won't be necessary." The man reached into his jacket pocket, pulled out a paper, and thrust it in her hand. "Summons to appear in court. No need to get angry. Just doing my job."

Cora felt the need to get angry. "What!?" she thundered, erupting from her chair.

"You low-life son of a bitch! To ambush me at the bridge table! At a game I'm actually winning! Of all the miserable, sneaky, low-down —"

The process server was evidently used to encountering reactions of this sort. Before Cora could even launch into her more vulgar constructions, the man was gone.

Cora followed him out into the parking lot, waving the summons and offering to put an end to his career as a process server forever unless he was able to figure out a way to serve subpoenas on the Internet by typing with his nose. She did not stop until the man's car rocketed out the driveway and disappeared into the night.

Cora went back inside, where her friends were commiserating over her bad fortune.

"What is it?" Iris Cooper asked.

"I don't know," Cora told her. "I'm too angry to read it."

"Let me," Iris said. She took the summons from Cora, smoothed it out, looked it over. "It appears to be a divorce complaint."

"A divorce complaint? How can it be a divorce complaint? I'm not *married!*"

"It's not a divorce complaint," Iris said.

"It's not? You just said it was."

"I thought it was. It reads pretty much the same. But the guy doesn't want a divorce.

46

He wants an annulment."

"An annulment!" Cora said. "That's ridiculous! I may not remember all my marriages, but I damn sure never had one that wasn't consummated. Who is this jerk?"

"Let's see." Iris flipped the page. "Ah, here we are. A Mr. Melvin Crabtree."

Cora's mouth fell open.

CHAPTER 8

Sherry couldn't believe it. "Melvin?"

"Yes."

"Your fifth husband?"

Cora waggled her fingers. "Give or take."

"Cora."

"Well, there's a gray area."

"As I recall, you didn't like Melvin."

"Your recollection is correct. Actually, I didn't like any of my husbands, but for Melvin I had a particular loathing."

"You didn't like any of your husbands?"

"Oh, when I married them I did. Otherwise, why would I? Unless they were particularly rich."

"You're not really that cynical," Sherry said. "You're just talking tough because you're scared."

"Why, Sherry Carter, are you lecturing me? I swear, you're acting very maternal."

"That joke's getting stale. You know

perfectly well I've been lecturing you for years."

"It's nice to hear you finally admit it."

"You're doing everything in your power to avoid talking about Melvin."

"I'm doing everything in my power to avoid *Melvin*. The man was out of my life, and here he is, back to haunt me. Even if it is only on a sheet of paper."

"Will he be in court?"

"How the hell should I know. *I* didn't expect to be in court."

"You show this to Becky Baldwin?"

"No. I brought it home to show you."

"I think you need a lawyer. Why don't you ask Becky to represent you."

"She'd probably want me to pay her."

"Lawyers do like to be paid."

"Damn it."

"What's the big deal, Cora? You got some money from your book sales."

"Yes. Along with my alimony, it keeps me going."

"So what's the problem?"

"He wants to stop my alimony."

"Melvin's paying you alimony?"

"Of course he is. You think I'd let that son of a bitch get off scot-free?"

"Of course you wouldn't."

"Not that it's princely. Twelve hundred a

49

month doesn't go nearly as far these days. I was actually thinking of asking the judge to increase it."

"And Melvin wants it stopped?"

"Of course he does."

"On what grounds?"

"That I have another husband living."

Sherry's eyes widened. "Chester T. Markowitz?"

Cora waggled her finger. "Don't look at me like that."

"Like what?"

"You know like what. Like 'I told you so.' "

"I was not looking at you like that."

"What were you doing?"

"All right, I *was* looking at you like that. Don't you think you deserve it?"

"Right, right. Kick a person when they're down."

"Cora, if you really stand to lose twelve hundred a month, isn't it worth spending some of it on a lawyer to see that it doesn't happen?"

"I know. It's just the principle of the thing. The thought that Melvin would cost me a penny."

"Well, you're costing him quite a bit."

"And he deserves every cent. Oh, my God, Sherry. If you had any *idea* what that man was like. It wasn't just the cheating and throwing it in my face and undermining me to my friends behind my back. Or making fun of my cooking."

"You cooked?"

"Don't start with me. The son of a bitch *made* me cook. Wheedled and cajoled me into cooking. Then ridiculed me for it. As he did everything else."

"Everything else?"

"I don't care to discuss it. The man was a master manipulator. Never laid a finger on me, I'll give him that. But he could be the most sinister son of a bitch this side of the Marquis de Sade. I tell you, twelve hundred a month is a slap on the wrist. I wouldn't go through it again for five grand."

"You must have liked him at one time."

"Of course I liked him. He was a fascinating, charismatic bad boy. He's the one who taught me to shoot, for God's sake. Utterly irresistible, as long as he was being a bad boy to somebody else."

"You broke up his marriage."

"Did I say that?"

"But you did, didn't you? You were the other woman."

Cora made a face. "Well, of course it sounds bad when you say it like that."

"You liked being the other woman. Beating the wife's time. It didn't occur to you

51

there'd be *another* other woman and the wife would be you."

"Are you *trying* to piss me off?"

Sherry's eyes twinkled. "So, you don't like it when a person won't stop teasing you?"

Cora smoldered in silence.

"You really haven't been married since Melvin?"

"I almost was."

"Oh. Right."

Cora's last engagement had ended badly. It coincided with her stopping drinking. Cora hadn't come close to the altar since. Sherry wondered if there was a connection. She wasn't about to point it out.

"So, marrying would have stopped Melvin's alimony. A good reason to stay single."

"Not the only one," Cora said. "You get married, the first thing you know you're knocked up and trying to deny it."

Sherry ignored the jab. "Nice try. The topic is your ex-husband. Which is somewhat ironic. When we started living together, the topic was *my* ex-husband. But Dennis has been a good boy lately. Haven't heard from him in months."

"What am I going to do?" Cora said.

"Only one thing I can think of."

"What's that?"

Sherry smiled. "Why don't we put *my*

picture on the Puzzle Lady column, and *I'll* pretend I write it, so *you* can hide from *your* abusive ex-husband."

CHAPTER 9

Becky Baldwin could have passed for a Victoria's Secret model. Men wanting to hire her were hopelessly torn. They liked the idea of having her around but doubted that anyone who looked like her could know any law.

They would be wrong. Becky Baldwin was as sharp as they came, probably could have made partner in some prestigious law firm, if she could have stood working for someone. But Becky liked calling her own shots.

She looked up from reading the summons.

"Well?" Cora said.

"This isn't good."

"I don't need a lawyer to tell me that."

"I always like to make the circumstances seem dire before I jack up my fee."

"I'm not amused, Becky."

"I wasn't joking. This is a court appearance with a lot of money involved. If I win, I get mine."

"You're taking it on contingency?"

"Yes, wouldn't that be nice. I'm taking it on retainer *against* contingency. You pay me to go to court. If I win, you pay me more."

"Since when did you get so hard-nosed?"

"There's a lot of money involved. Your alimony is twelve hundred forty-three bucks. That's more than the monthly rent on my office and apartment combined. And your books are selling."

"How do you know that?"

"Amazon.com. When you called for the appointment, I logged on and checked your numbers. You're doing very well indeed."

"Great," Cora said. "So how do I win the case?"

"I don't know. It seems you rather injudiciously accepted a check for ten thousand dollars from a man you never met."

"You think I should have turned it down?"

"I thought you were good at math. Or is it just putting numbers in a line? Your alimony is nearly twelve hundred fifty bucks a month. Times two would be twenty-five hundred. Times four would be five thousand. Times eight would be ten thousand. So, you tell me. Is it worth ten thousand dollars to give up your alimony?"

"I bet when you add in your fee it isn't."

"My fee is to keep that from happening."

"Oh? I thought it was just to go to court. The *contingency* was for stopping that from happening."

"If you'd prefer to hire some other lawyer . . ."

"Did I say that?"

"Relax, Cora. You've been in worse scrapes than this. You always come up with something. How come this time you can't think clearly?"

"This time it's Melvin."

"Oh."

Cora's eyes narrowed. "What do you mean by that?"

"You still have feelings for him."

Cora scowled, took out a pack of cigarettes.

"No smoking."

"You wanna needle me about my ex-husband, I'm gonna smoke."

"So you do have *feelings* for him."

"I have feelings, and they're not kind. The man made my life a living hell."

"In what way?"

"Why?"

"Why? Don't be silly. If that man's going to try to get your alimony reduced, I need all the ammunition I can get."

"He's not trying to get it reduced. He's trying to get it stopped."

"Same thing."

"The hell it is! He's not saying I deserve less, he's saying he shouldn't be paying at all!"

"I understand the situation."

"So why does it matter what a creep he is?"

"It always matters. If this goes to the jury —"

"Jury! What the hell do you mean, jury? Alimony's up to the judge."

"Yes, but if there are criminal charges . . ."

"Criminal! Now see here! I came in with a simple property settlement, you're blowing it up into the trial of the century."

"That's a bit of an exaggeration."

"Well, the century just started." Cora strode to the door, stepped out in the stairwell, lit her cigarette. Becky's office was on the second floor over a pizza parlor. It was early Friday morning, but they were already open. The smell of smoke mingled with the smell of pepperoni.

"I'm not trying to scare you, Cora. But if this guy's a jerk, he's going to pull out all the stops. Obtaining money under false pretenses is not looked on kindly by the courts."

"That's why it's up to you to show it didn't happen. Not that I should get off lightly because my ex-husband's a creep."

"Of course. And that's what I'm going to do. In the meantime, humor me. Tell me about Melvin."

Cora exhaled a cloud of smoke. "I met him in Vegas. My marriage had fallen apart, I was drowning my sorrows in settlement money. Not really drowning my sorrows — more like taking a victory lap. I was playing poker. Seven-card stud. He was at the table. I probably wouldn't have noticed him at all, except he folded a winning hand."

"What do you mean?"

"I bluffed, and he folded a winner."

"How do you know he had a winner?"

"He had me beat on board."

"Huh?"

"Stick with law, kid. Anyway, he said, 'Nice hand, little lady.' He smiled. Slimy son of a bitch."

"Never mind the slimy part. That came later. You liked him then. How come?"

"He was an attractive man. Wavy hair, flashing eyes, lovely smile, good teeth."

"Oh."

"The teeth were capped, the hair was plugs, the eyes were roving. Complete phony. I should have known."

"What did he do?"

Cora snorted. "Rat bastard bought me a drink."

"That's not so bad."

"He was there with his wife."

"Oh." Becky considered. "That's good."

"How is that good?"

"If he was cheating on his wife, I can raise the inference he was cheating on you. It never hurts to stir the pot of marital infidelity."

"You speaking as a lawyer?"

"How else would I be speaking?"

"Aaron just got married."

"Aaron is not my first ex-boyfriend to get married."

"Hmm. Bad track record?"

"Finish your cigarette and come back in. We don't really need to discuss this where the people in the pizza parlor can hear."

"You didn't mind discussing *my* life where the people in the pizza parlor can hear."

"You don't run a business over the pizza parlor. Come in when you're done."

Cora stubbed out her cigarette, flipped it out the window. She went in to find Becky sitting at her desk. "Gee. I scared you back into stuffy lawyer mode."

Becky ignored the comment, poised a pencil over a legal pad. "So, you met him in

Vegas. How soon after that were you married?"

"About six months."

"That long?"

"Well, he had to get a divorce."

"Of course. Silly me. Are you sure he did?"

"Why?"

"Be interesting if he hadn't. The guy's going to throw another husband at you, you could throw another wife at him."

"What good would that do?"

"We're trying to put you in the better light. These are our talking points. Husbands cheat. Men are pigs. He did cheat on you, didn't he?"

"He cheated on the honeymoon."

"Can you prove it?"

"Yeah, if you can subpoena some nameless cocktail waitress who worked some nightclub in New York."

"*Some* nightclub?"

"People drink in nightclubs. Things get fuzzy."

"Great." Becky sighed. "All right. Let me ask you the money question."

"What's that?"

"We have to be in court at ten o'clock Monday morning." Becky cocked her head. "If Melvin is there, can you stop yourself from jumping up and yelling at him?"

"Becky."

"I'm serious. If I'm going to be your lawyer, you have to do what I say. You have to sit there and be quiet. Can you do that?"

"Yeah," Cora said grudgingly.

"You won't jump up and yell at him?"

"No."

"No what?"

"No, I won't jump up and yell at him."

Becky exhaled. "Good."

"I might shoot him."

CHAPTER 10

Melvin wasn't there. By ten o'clock Monday morning the only one at the plaintiff's table was a rather smarmy-looking lawyer, a short, balding, sweating man with sideburns much too long for his age and furtive, darting eyes. He was, Cora saw at a glance, someone she would never marry. Considering her current lack of male companionship, that was saying something.

Cora, seated next to Becky Baldwin, was dressed in her most conservative, respectable outfit. Becky, on the other hand, was dressed like a million bucks. Her outfit seemed to scream that here was the femme fatale who lured men to their financial ruin, as opposed to her prim and proper client. Cora understood the strategy but didn't appreciate it.

Judge Hobbs banged the court to order. He reviewed the next case on the docket, then stared skeptically down at the plaintiff's attorney. "Let me be sure I understand this. This is a petition for annulment?"

"That's right."

"The plaintiff is seeking to annul a marriage that took place over fifteen years ago?"

"Yes, Your Honor."

"On what grounds?"

"At the time of the marriage, the defendant already had a husband living."

"Is the former husband living now?"

"No, Your Honor."

"Then he can't testify. And the plaintiff isn't here."

"No, Your Honor."

"So he can't testify either. Your petition would seem to have no grounds. Do you have witnesses to the marriage?"

"I don't need witnesses, Your Honor. I expect to prove the marriage by the defendant herself."

"The defendant herself? I find that hard to believe. Ms. Baldwin, is your client prepared to concede the marriage?"

"Absolutely not, Your Honor."

"Is your client prepared to testify that she had a husband living at the time she entered into marriage with the plaintiff?"

"No, Your Honor."

"There you are. It would appear, Mr. Fleckstein, that no one is prepared to testify to your contention."

"Not so, Your Honor. I have evidence."

"What kind of evidence?"

"Physical evidence."

"You have a marriage license?"

"Yes, Your Honor."

"Between the defendant and her previous husband?"

"No, Your Honor. Between the defendant and the plaintiff."

"What about her prior husband?"

"He's dead, Your Honor."

"I mean the marriage license."

"Well, I can't ask him to produce it if he's dead. And I doubt if the defendant will produce one."

"The defendant will not," Becky Baldwin said.

"In which case I would be inclined to dismiss the petition."

Cora beamed like a contented cat.

"I have other evidence, Your Honor."

"What evidence?"

"Evidence the defendant admitted to her marriage with her prior husband."

"That would be hearsay," Judge Hobbs said.

"Actually, I believe it would be an admission against interest. However, I am not talking about a verbal admission. I have physical evidence that the defendant acknowledged the relationship. If I may be allowed to present it."

"You have the evidence in court?"

"Yes, Your Honor."

"Very well. Make your showing."

"I will need to call a witness."

"For what purpose?"

"To identify the evidence."

"Is the witness here in court?"

"Yes, Your Honor."

"Very well. Call your witness."

"Call Roger Randolph."

Cora glared as the banker made his way to the witness stand. He did not meet her eyes. His manner seemed reluctant. Cora didn't give a damn. If the son of a bitch testified against her, she'd be damned if she was solving his break-in.

"Your name is Roger Randolph?"

"That's right."

"You work at the First National Bank?"

"Yes."

"What do you do there?"

"I approve loans."

Cora rolled her eyes. Even in court the banker described himself as the benevolent giver of money. She wondered if that constituted perjury.

"You have other functions at the bank?"

"Yes, of course. I'm a manager. I monitor transactions, assist the tellers with any problems."

Cora gnashed her teeth, wondered how much the tellers appreciated his officious meddling.

"The tellers come to you when they have problems?"

"That's right."

Becky Baldwin was on her feet. "We will stipulate the man is a saint. Is there a point to this?"

"There certainly is. Mr. Randolph, do you recall an occasion last week when a teller asked you to approve a check?"

"Yes, I do. One of our tellers brought me a check that had been deposited for collection. She wanted to know if it was all right."

"Mr. Randolph, I hand you a check and ask you if it is the one you are referring to."

The banker took the check, looked it over. "Yes, it is."

"And who is the check made out to?"

"Cora Felton Markowitz."

"Cora Felton Markowitz?"

"That's right."

"Do you know a Cora Felton Markowitz?"

"I don't know a Cora Felton Markowitz. I know Cora Felton, of course. She's sitting right there."

"But you don't know if she's the woman who presented the check."

"Well, according to the teller —"

The little lawyer put up his hand. "That would be hearsay, Mr. Randolph. The teller will speak for herself. So, the check was made out to a Cora Felton Markowitz. And on whose account was the check drawn?"

"The check was from the account of Fleckstein and Stone, conservators for the estate of the late Chester T. Markowitz."

"And what is the amount of the check?"

"Ten thousand dollars."

"And why did the teller bring it to you?"

"She said —"

Fleckstein held up his hand. "Never mind what she said. Just tell us what concerned her about the check."

"There was typing on the back of the check above the endorsement. It was somewhat unusual. The teller wanted to be sure it was all right."

"There is typing on the back of that check?"

"Yes, there is."

"Could you read it for us, please."

Mr. Randolph read from the check. " 'I, Cora Felton Markowitz, do hereby agree that the amount of this check, to wit ten

67

thousand dollars, represents the entire amount of the inheritance specified and/or implied in the last will and testament of my husband, Chester T. Markowitz, and I hereby relinquish any and all claims on any and all moneys which might be discovered to be part of the estate of the said Chester T. Markowitz.' "

"Your Honor, we offer the check in evidence. If the defendant is not willing to stipulate she is the one who endorsed it Cora Felton Markowitz, we offer to produce a handwriting expert to so testify."

"The defense is not going to stipulate a thing," Becky said.

Fleckstein nodded as if that were exactly what he expected and turned back to the witness. "Was there a deposit slip with the check?"

"Yes, there was."

"To whose account was the check deposited?"

"To the account of Cora Felton."

"Not Cora Felton Markowitz?"

"No, just Cora Felton."

"You saw nothing wrong with depositing Cora Felton Markowitz's check to Cora Felton?"

"No."

"Why not?"

"It is common practice for women using their maiden names to receive checks made out in their married ones. Particularly in the case of women no longer living with their husbands. Such checks are deposited to their accounts as a matter of course."

"And you assumed that — Withdraw the question. The fact is, the check was deposited to the account of Cora Felton?"

"That's right."

"Do you know Cora Felton personally?"

"Yes, I do."

"Is she in the courtroom?"

"Yes, she is. She's the woman sitting with her attorney at the defense table."

"There you are, Your Honor," Fleckstein said.

Judge Hobbs considered. "Ms. Baldwin, do you have any evidence to refute the presentation made by the plaintiff?"

"Frankly, I'm not sure, Your Honor," Becky said. "If I might have a short adjournment?"

Judge Hobbs smiled. This was exactly what he always hoped for in a marital dispute. The attorneys would take a recess and work out a settlement out of court. "Very well. It would appear that there is at least sufficient grounds to proceed with this complaint. So let's take a recess, and we will pick this up at . . ." Judge Hobbs checked the docket. "Tomorrow's no good. Let's see. Wednesday. Ten o'clock Wednesday morning."

Lennie Fleckstein grinned triumphantly and glanced over his shoulder at the back of the courtroom.

Bad move.

Cora Felton, who was glaring at the little attorney and fantasizing elaborate methods of open heart surgery she might perform without anesthesia, naturally followed his gaze.

Silhouetted in the light streaming in the doorway was the shadow of a man leaving the courtroom. He was of average height. His body was lean, but not skinny. His stance was sure, solid, athletic. A fedora was perched on his head at a rakish angle. His jaw jutted out aggressively, challenging the world, but the outline of his lips was a cocky grin.

Cora sucked in her breath.

Melvin.

CHAPTER 11

Cora came out of the courthouse and
looked around. Melvin was nowhere to be
seen. That figured. The slimy son of a bitch
was as elusive as ever. Cora could recall
once on her honeymoon Melvin had gone
out for a pack of cigarettes and been gone
for five hours. It was only later she found
out he didn't smoke.

Becky Baldwin followed Cora out. "Hey,
I'm sorry you didn't like the ruling, but we
didn't expect to win today."

"I was looking for Melvin."

"Melvin wasn't here."

"Yes, he was. He was hiding in the back. I
saw him slip out after Hobbs adjourned
court."

"Are you sure?"

"No. And that's just like him, to make me
doubt my own senses."

It occurred to Becky that if Melvin wasn't
here, he could hardly be blamed for doing

that, but she figured it wasn't a good time to point that out.

People were pouring out of the courthouse now. Melvin's attorney was among them.

Cora's eyes blazed. "Hey, shyster, was that your client hiding in the back?"

"I *beg* your pardon?"

"What my client meant to say," Becky amended hastily, "was she congratulates you on an excellent presentation of your case, and wonders if your client happened to be present."

Lennie Fleckstein had been prepared to take Cora Felton's attorney down a peg, but Becky Baldwin's charm was not lost on him. He smiled and said, "The seat next to me appeared to be empty."

"Some clients are shy. Like to stay in the background."

"I notice your client doesn't."

"Let's not discuss my client."

"And yet you want to discuss mine. That hardly seems fair."

"Hey! I'm standing right here," Cora said.

"And I'm speaking for you as your attorney." Becky pointed to Aaron Grant, who was hovering nearby. "Why don't you talk to your niece's husband. He could probably use a story." She frowned. "On second thought, that's not such a great idea, either.

Why don't you go construct a crossword puzzle."

"Yeah, like that's gonna happen," Cora muttered. "You wanna act like my attorney, fine. Ask him if his client's here. It's a simple yes-or-no question. All this legal double-talk is just the slimy evasions of —"

"I think I'd like to jump in here," Becky said. "Mr. Fleckstein, I'm sure you've handled enough cases to realize that these matrimonial issues are not always amicable. I hope we can put this aside and discuss it as professionals."

"That would be nice."

"There's a restaurant just outside of town. The Country Kitchen. Are you familiar with it?"

"Is that the one that looks like a big log cabin?"

"That's the place. Meet you in the bar?"

"Half an hour."

"Perfect."

As the little attorney hurried off, Cora turned on her own lawyer. "What the hell do you think you're doing?"

"Oh, come on, Cora. You've been divorced before. You know the drill."

"Yeah, I've been divorced before. But I was the one doing the divorcing. I've never been the goddamned defendant."

"The process is the same."

"The hell it is. The process is showing the son of a bitch I married is a lying, cheating weasel. This is nothing at all like that. Melvin's trying to prove I lied to him."

"Did you?"

"Of *course* I lied to him. He was my husband."

"That's probably not the way you want to answer that in court."

"We're not *in* court." Cora shook her head. "Why are you having lunch with the sleazeball lawyer?"

"I got a chance to sound him out, see what he's got. I'd be a damn fool not to take it."

"Sound him out, hell. You couldn't even get him to admit Melvin's here."

"And that's what this is all about, isn't it? The fact that it's Melvin. Look, I don't know what kind of relationship you had with this guy, and I don't wanna know, but the fact is he pushes your buttons. That's not good. If it happens in front of a judge, it's gonna cost you money."

"Everything costs me money," Cora groused. "Hell, I bet you're gonna charge me for your damn lunch."

CHAPTER 12

Lennie Fleckstein had a grilled ham-and-cheese sandwich with French fries and a stein of beer.

Becky Baldwin had a field greens salad with vinaigrette and a sugarless iced tea. It was not her usual lunch. Becky was perfectly capable of eating her way through a cheeseburger and onion rings and ate like a bird only when she wanted to emphasize how much she looked like a supermodel. Not that she had any interest in the man. But in what she imagined would be a difficult negotiation, there was no reason not to take advantage of her allure.

Becky smiled at the little attorney. "So, I'm not sure I understand your position in all this."

"What do you mean?"

"The check you presented in court. From the law firm of Fleckstein and Stone, attorneys for the late Chester T. Markowitz."

"What about it?"

"Would that happen to be your law firm?"

"As a matter of fact, it would."

"You are attorney for Chester T. Markowitz?"

"The estate of Chester T. Markowitz, yes."

"The man you claim is Cora Felton's ex-husband."

"There's no *ex* about it. Unless you're aware of some divorce I'm not familiar with."

"The man is dead."

"True."

"That would seem to make him an *ex*-husband."

"It's a fine legal point. We should probably save it for the judge."

"That's not really where I was going," Becky said. "The point is, you're attorney for one of my client's ex-husbands. And here you are, representing another."

"You're admitting Mr. Markowitz is your client's ex-husband?"

"*Alleged* ex-husband," Becky said. "You're not recording this conversation, are you?"

"Heavens, no."

"If you were, I would insist on you playing this part of it, where I explain that I have made no such admission."

"Not a problem. I was speaking casually, too."

Lennie sipped his beer.

Becky nibbled at her salad. "I notice how artfully you changed the subject to avoid giving me an answer."

"About what?"

"The fact you're representing both men. Chester T. Markowitz and Melvin Crabtree. Isn't that a conflict of interest?"

Lennie smiled. "Mr. Markowitz's interests could hardly conflict with those of Mr. Crabtree."

"How about collusion, then?"

"Dead men don't collude."

"I think a judge will want more than that."

"More than what?"

"Your bland assurance that everything is hunky-dory."

"Fine. We'll take it up then."

"You wouldn't care to explain, just talking casually?"

"I'm not sure how casually we can talk, what with you worrying about conversations being recorded."

"Speaking casually or not, is your client in town?"

"I have no idea."

"My client thinks she saw him."

"Then you know more than I do."

"That's a strange position for a lawyer involved in a lawsuit. I would think you'd keep track of your client."

"Not so much a problem, in the age of cell phones. I can call him if I need him."

"Convenient."

"Isn't it? What do you care where my client is, anyway?"

"I can't wait to get him on the stand."

Fleckstein smiled. "Be my guest."

CHAPTER 13

"Pine Ridge Motel? I'd like to leave a message for Melvin Crabtree."

"Who?"

"Melvin Crabtree. He's staying there. I'd like to leave a message."

"There's no Melvin Crabtree registered here."

"Oh. Thank you."

Cora hung up, checked the Yellow Pages, dialed again.

"Hello? Four Seasons Motel? I'd like to leave a message for Melvin Crabtree."

Cora listened, slammed down the phone.

Damn. Only one more motel. If he wasn't there, she'd have to try the bed-and-breakfasts. And there were a zillion of them.

"Hello? Oakwood Motel? I'd like to leave a message for Melvin Crabtree."

The motel manager sounded cranky and put-upon. "Why don't you ring his room?"

Bingo!

"I would, but I forgot which room he's in."

"One oh five," the manager said, and hung up.

Cora didn't ring Melvin's room. She drove out there.

There was no car in front of 105. She knocked on the door anyway, but there was no answer.

Damn. If he was out driving around, there was no way to find him.

Cora frowned. What was she saying? What was the matter with her? Just because it was Melvin, she wasn't thinking straight. Put him out of your mind. It isn't the ex-husband from hell. It's just someone you want to find.

Cora picked up the phone, called the police station.

Dan Finley was manning the desk. "Baker-haven police. Officer Finley speaking."

"Hey, Dan, it's Cora. What you up to?"

"You kidding me?"

"Just curious."

"Well, let's see. I've done my daily cross-word puzzle, downloaded the latest police briefings, and now I'm reading a book."

"How's your pull with the New York car rental companies?"

"Why?"

"I want you to trace a rental for me."

"Is this police business?"

"Of course."

"Then why isn't Chief Harper bringing it to me?"

"Probably too busy."

"So he asked you to ask me?"

"That's a clumsy way to phrase it."

"What's a good way to phrase it?"

"You're too quick for me today, Dan. I need to find out if Melvin Crabtree rented a car recently. If so, I need the make and plate."

"Isn't Melvin Crabtree the ex-husband making trouble for you in court?"

"Oh my. That would be quite a co-incidence, wouldn't it?"

"It certainly would."

"Don't string me along, Dan. If you don't want to do it, just say so."

Dan got back to her in twenty minutes. "Cream-colored Lexus. New York plate, BFH561."

"That was fast, Dan."

"Well, what with it being official police business and all."

Cora went out, got in her car, and cruised the streets of Bakerhaven, looking for a cream-colored Lexus.

She'd just passed the police station when

81

Becky Baldwin ran out and waved her arms.

Cora pulled to a stop. "Whaddya want?"

"I've been trying to get in touch with you. I had lunch with Melvin's attorney."

"Oh? What did you have?"

Becky gave her a look. "Are you deliberately trying to be irritating?"

"Yeah, I guess so. When you start collaborating with the enemy."

"I thought you wanted to know if Melvin was in town."

"Yeah. Did you find out?"

"No."

"I suppose lunch will appear on your expense account anyway."

"Cora."

"Relax. I did the work for you. Melvin's in town. Driving a cream-colored Lexus. If you see him, flag me down again."

"How did you find out?"

"Simple detective work. Why are you so het up over lunch?"

"There's a weak point in Melvin's case. The attorney's representing him *and* Chester T. Markowitz. That reeks to high heaven."

"What's the shyster say about it?"

"He won't say. I think we can make something out of it."

"Damn."

"What's the matter?"

"I don't like it. Here's a clear-cut case, and you're resorting to technicalities."

"What's so clear-cut about it?"

"I never knew any Chester T. Markowitz."

"And yet you cashed his check."

"Shut up."

Cora continued to zigzag in and out of the side streets, a circuitous route that eventually led her to the outskirts of town. The local shopping mall was only a mile down the road. She checked it out on a hunch. A bad hunch. Melvin wasn't parked in front of the Starbucks. Or the Stop & Shop. Or the Bed Bath & Beyond.

Cora pulled out of the mall parking lot and headed back toward town, following a different circuitous route from the one that had taken her there.

She almost zoomed right by the antiques shop. It wasn't one she'd ever stopped at before, but then there were nearly as many antiques shops as there were bed-and-breakfasts in Bakerhaven. This one was called Ye Olde Antique Shop, old spelled with an *e*, as if the archaic spelling would make the goods inside even more antique.

A cream-colored Lexus was parked outside. It had no license plate on the front. Cora had to back up half a block to check the one in the rear. Sure enough, the plate was BFH561.

Cora pulled up behind the Lexus and got out.

Two men came around the corner of the shop.

One was the owner. A little old man with horn-rimmed glasses, white hair, and a blue polo shirt.

The man next to him was short, stocky, but still athletically built. His brown curls were flecked with gray, but his chin jutted out, firm, assertive. He wore no glasses. His blue eyes were keen. His lip was twisted in a sardonic smile.

Cora felt her pulse quicken.

She stepped across the sidewalk to intercept the men in the middle of the lawn.

Melvin saw her coming. He stopped. His chin came up. His lips twisted in a haughty sneer. "Well, well, well."

Cora plunged her hand into her drawstring purse.

Melvin stopped. The smile froze on his face. He actually flinched. After all, he was the one who had taught Cora to shoot.

But it was not a gun Cora wrenched from her purse, merely a pack of cigarettes.

Melvin's jaw relaxed. Still, he balanced on the balls of his feet. He looked ready to spring in any direction.

"Well, Melvin," Cora said. She tapped out a cigarette, lit it up. "Want one? Oh, that's right. You don't smoke."

Melvin cocked his head, grinned. "So, you tracked me down. Quite the little detective, aren't you, sweetie? I always liked that about you."

"Yeah, until I found those hotel receipts."

"Why dwell on the past? Let bygones be bygones."

"Easy for you to say. Why are you doing this?"

"Why am I doing what?"

"Don't play games. I'm not in the mood."

"You think it's fair I pay you twelve hundred bucks a month *not* to be my wife?"

"It is considering what I put up with when I was."

"It's been a long time."

"Murder never outlaws, Melvin."

"I didn't murder anyone."

"Just an example. What makes you think you can get away with it?"

"Get away with what?"

"This scam."

"Scam? What scam? Are you telling me you haven't been married since we've been divorced?"

"It was a cheap trick, Melvin. And the

judge knows it."

"Cheap trick. I'll tell you what's a cheap trick. Collecting alimony you're not entitled to."

"You know damn well I'm entitled to it."

"I know nothing of the sort. I'm an honest man. I go by the letter of the law. The law says if you marry again, I'm off the hook."

"I didn't marry again."

"That's not the way my lawyer sees it."

"Your lawyer is a two-bit shyster."

"Whoa! You're lucky I'm a nice guy. A hard-ass would try to drum up a damage suit."

"Yeah, Melvin. You're a real nice guy. The ladies love you, don't they?"

"Some do. I'm sorry you're no longer in that group."

"Would you really expect me to be?"

"Hey, we had some good times."

"Everyone has good times, Melvin, or they wouldn't get married. It's what happens after."

Melvin's smile was roguish. "It was pretty good."

"Don't start with me."

The antiques dealer, embarrassed and flustered, couldn't wait to get out of there. "If you need me, I'll be inside."

Melvin was grinning. "You're still crazy about me, aren't you?"

Cora shook her head. "I don't know how you live with yourself."

"That's an evasion."

"Yes, it is. I'm trying to avoid pulling my gun out and shooting you dead."

"That's hardly fair. I taught you to shoot."

"Only one of your big mistakes."

"You're quick as you ever were. That's what I liked about you. A good sparring partner. You always could give as good as you got."

"Forget it, Melvin. I'm not interested."

"Oh, no? Then why'd you hunt me down?"

"Huh?"

"You weren't just driving by. You were obviously looking for me. When you stopped, I was nowhere in sight. You must have spotted my car. Which means you knew what kind of car I was driving. Which means you *found out* what kind of car I was driving. Which is not that easy to do. You must have gone to some trouble to find out what kind of car I was driving. Which means you were looking for me. And I'm wondering why?"

"Why do you even ask that? You're here making trouble for me. You think I'm going to take it lying down?"

Melvin rolled his eyes, grinned. "Oh, what a straight line."

"I'm warning you, Melvin."

"You're warning me? What are you warning me about? You gonna kill me? You gonna take me for more money? Come on, Cora. The fact you went to so much trouble to find me proves just one thing. You can't leave me alone."

"Yeah, right, Melvin," Cora said sarcastically. "I was really hoping for a reconciliation. Of course, you're probably married, aren't you? You were always married to someone or another."

"Come on, Cora. Considering the amount of time we were married, don't you think the alimony's a little high?"

"Considering the amount of physical and mental cruelty, I'd say it's rather low."

"Physical?"

"You never pushed me around?"

"As I recall, you beat the hell out of me."

"You think you didn't deserve it?"

"God, you're a spitfire."

Cora exhaled in frustration, actually stamped her foot. Her face was red.

A blond woman came out the front door of the antiques shop. She sized up the situation, slipped her arm through Melvin's, and spoke to him, though her eyes never left

Cora's face. "So, sweetie. Who's your friend?"

CHAPTER 14

She was young. That was the first strike against her. She was with Melvin. That was the second. And she was looking at Cora the way one might regard particularly odoriferous pond scum.

Cora didn't wait for an explanation. "I'm sweetie's ex-wife. Ex as in not anymore, it's all over, get me out of here."

The blonde's baby blue eyes were not kind. "You're the leech who's bleeding him dry?"

"Gee, I didn't quite catch that. Would you care to repeat it for my attorney to process?"

The blonde made a face men probably thought was cute but which made Cora want to punch her lights out. She side-spied up at Melvin. "You were married to *that?*"

Melvin knew the remark wasn't going to sit well. He managed to place himself between the two women, not a particularly comfortable position, and glanced nervously from one to the other. "Ladies, my lawyer would be most unhappy to have this conversation take place in his absence."

Cora suggested activities with which Melvin's lawyer could occupy himself in his absence, many of which would have been illegal in most states.

The blonde looked at her in mock shock. "Kiss your mother with that mouth?"

Cora shook her head disparagingly. "I don't think you wanna talk mothers, dearie. You're out of your league."

"Fine. We'll keep this civilized," blondie said. "The fact is you're older than I thought. Melvin still shouldn't have to wait for you to die. It's your fault he doesn't have the money to treat me the way I deserve. It's your fault we're in a crummy room in a crummy motel, when we should be able to afford a luxury suite. It's your fault we're here in this hick town trying to raise the cash to take a cruise, instead of lying on the beach in some island in the Bahamas."

Melvin looked at her placatingly. "Bambi . . ."

Cora's eyebrows launched into orbit. "Bambi?" Her smile was enormous. "Is she really Bambi?" She quoted, " 'Man has entered the forest.' "

The blonde lowered her finger at Cora.

"All right. I've had just about enough out of you."

"Have you really?" Cora cocked her head. "What do you plan to do about it?"

"Are you kidding me? You think I can't take an old lady?"

"I'm sure you can." Cora reached in her drawstring purse, pulled out her gun. "Go ahead. Make my day."

Bambi's mouth fell open.

"Damn, that's not my cigarettes. I keep doing that." Cora looked back at the young blonde. "Now then, what were you saying?"

Bambi was falling all over herself backing up and hiding behind Melvin. "You're crazy. You're out of your mind."

"Oh yeah?" Cora grinned. "That doesn't speak very well of you. Taunting an armed, crazy woman." She shoved the gun back in her purse.

A police car pulled up, and Officer Dan Finley got out. He looked rather uncomfortable as he approached the group. "Ah, hi."

Cora looked at him. "Hi? That's your official police greeting? Hi?"

"Well, I'm not on official police business." He looked at Melvin. "Would this be Mr. Melvin Crabtree?"

"Yes, it would," Cora said helpfully. "And this is Bambi."

"You're adversarial parties in a lawsuit?"

"That's right," Melvin said. "I fail to see what business that is of the police."

"Absolutely none, you're quite right. However, it is my job as a policeman to keep the peace. And airing legal matters outside of court can sometimes lead to public recriminations which —"

"Good God, Dan. You sound like a walking thesaurus. What are you trying to say?"

"The chief indicated," Dan said pointedly to Cora, "that I've been busy lately, and he would hate for me to get tied up by a domestic dispute escalating out of control." He put up his hands. "Not to imply that either party was apt to fly out of control. On the other hand, I have never met this gentleman, and the chief felt that in matrimonial issues —"

"For Christ's sake, Dan, give it a rest, or I'll side with Melvin. How about it, Mel? Think we could take this flatfoot?"

Cora's manner was jaunty as she uttered the phrase, but the moment it was out of her mouth, her face froze.

Melvin, who'd lined up beside her against the cop, was equally embarrassed.

Bambi was floored. Her jaw slack, she gaped at the two, realizing for the first time what they had once seen in each other.

Cora recovered first. "Sure, Dan. Wouldn't wanna make any trouble for you."

She turned and walked back to her car. Her face was flushed, her breath was coming fast. A torrent of conflicting emotions washed over her. It was nothing, she told herself, just the heat of the moment. That and the fact she hadn't had a man in months, the pickings in Bakerhaven being slim. And quitting drinking had cut down on her social life. Alcohol had always made her more social, less inhibited. Not that she ever was inhibited, but still. It also tended to improve the complexion of whatever inferior specimen of manhood was attempting to chat her up. In the absence of which most men looked none too good.

Not that Melvin did.

Damn it to hell!

Cora hopped in the car, slammed the door.

Before she could start the engine, Dan Finley stuck his head in the window. "Wanna follow me back to the station? Chief Harper wants to talk to you."

"I'll bet he does," Cora muttered.

CHAPTER 15

Chief Harper was in a benevolent, avuncular mood, particularly irritating since the man was younger than her. These days, Cora noted, almost *everyone* was younger than her. And that blond bitch of Melvin's. How old was she? Was she even out of *school?*

At any rate, Cora was ill disposed to listen to the chief's genial lecture.

"It's not that I don't understand," Harper said. "It's personal, it's upsetting, you're not yourself."

"I'm not myself?" Cora said icily.

"I'm trying to be nice."

"Yeah? Well, you're clearly no good at it."

"I'm trying to make allowances for your behavior."

"What's wrong with my behavior?"

"Nothing. I'm sure underneath you're your own sweet self. I'm referring to your tendency to regard the police department as your own personal investigative unit."

"Oh, come on, Chief. All this fuss over one lousy license plate number."

Harper frowned. "What license plate number?"

"You're not upset about a license plate number?"

"Why should I be upset about a license plate number?"

"No reason. So what are you upset about?"

"Never mind what I'm upset about. What's this about a license plate number?"

"Oh, for goodness' sake. What's Dan Finley been telling you?"

"Dan? What's Dan got to do with it?"

"Nothing, I'm sure. Chief, what the hell did you drag me in here for?"

"Becky Baldwin was by. Wanted to know if we could pull your ex-husband's rap sheet."

"Melvin's got a rap sheet?"

"I have no idea if Melvin has a rap sheet. Because I didn't pull it. Assuming he has one. Which I wouldn't know, because I didn't look. That's because I'm the chief of police and not a private investigator in the hire of your attorney."

"Of course. You couldn't be expected to look for Melvin's rap sheet." Cora kicked herself for not having been the one to think

96

of it. "But if you were going to pull it, how would you go about it?"

Harper took a breath. "Cora, I'm trying to indulge your loopy behavior because I understand you're under a lot of stress. But as far as your divorce hearing, I want nothing to do with it." He frowned. "Still, there's one thing bothers me."

"What's that?"

"Dan, hold down the front desk, will you? I'm going to have a little talk with Cora."

Chief Harper led Cora into his office and shut the door. He motioned her to a chair and sat behind his desk. "Now then. The banker who testified against you."

"Son of a bitch."

"Exactly. You seem pretty pissed off at him."

"Well, wouldn't you be?"

"All he said was you cashed the check. You did cash the check, didn't you?"

"I refuse to answer on advice of counsel."

"There you are. It's no revelation you cashed the check. Everyone knows you cashed the check. Whether you want to admit it or not."

"So?"

"Why are you so mad at the guy?"

"I'm not mad at him." Cora grimaced. "Well, yes, I am. I check out his so-called robbery and the next thing I know he's in court testifying against me."

"Do you think there's a connection?"

"Do you?"

"How could there be?"

"I don't know. Maybe the crook steals something valuable, says, 'If you don't testify the way I want, you'll never get it back.' "

"Of course he said nothing was stolen."

"What, you think he's gonna come out and say someone ripped him off for half a pound of heroin?"

"You think he's a drug pusher?"

"I don't know what I think. But I'm not about to give the guy a free pass. When I saw him take the stand, a little bird said, Why?"

"I don't suppose a subpoena had anything to do with it."

"Yeah, very funny. The point is, who knew to subpoena him? Did he come to Melvin, or did Melvin come to him?"

"I imagine it was Melvin's attorney who —"

"Yeah, yeah, yeah." Cora waved it away. "It's too pat, and I don't like it."

"What about the KenKen?"

"What about it?"

"You solved it. So tell me. What devastating revelation in the solution could lead an honest, upstanding bank manager to feel compelled to go to court and testify against a persecuted puzzle constructor?"

"My God, you're getting good with words, Chief. Maybe you should write my column."

"I'm serious. How is any of this the bank manager's fault?"

"I don't know, because I don't know all the facts. I just know Melvin's involved, so nothing can be taken at face value. He's a born liar, he's been practicing all his life, and he just gets better and better. If you want proof, take a look at his current wife."

"Current wife?"

"Yeah. He's tooling around town with her. At least he was. He probably dropped her off at day care."

"She has kids?"

"No."

Harper sighed. "Okay. I understand. The guy's trying to cut off your money and he's pushing his young wife in your face. This is why you have a lawyer. Because the lawyer isn't emotionally involved, and can think rationally. Except when your lawyer's as pushy as Becky Baldwin, she's apt to exceed her boundaries and try to tell me my job. But even so, she's got a firmer grip on the situation. When the bank manager testifies against you, she doesn't take it personally. She tries to see how much it damages your case, and what practical thing she can do about it. Which does not include beating the guy to a bloody pulp."

"I got it, I got it. You don't have to spell it out in words of one syllable. You're not talking to a two-year-old."

Harper grimaced, put up his hand. "Once again, in affairs of the heart —"

"This is not an affair of the heart! I hate the son of a bitch!"

Harper waited until the sound waves had finished reverberating through his office.

"Yeah, right."

CHAPTER 16

Cora confronted Becky Baldwin in her law office. "You went behind my back to the police?"

Becky frowned. "I don't know about anybody's back. I spoke to Chief Harper."

"About Melvin's rap sheet."

"That's right."

"You didn't think to run it by me first?"

"You don't think it's a good idea?"

"I'd just like to know what you're doing."

"I'm trying to win a court case. By any means possible. If you're quoting me to the media, by any *legal* means possible."

"Come on, Becky, can't you beat this case on the merits? Why do you have to drag Melvin's record into it?"

"He has a record?"

"I have no idea if he has a record. But a man of his many talents would have to be very lucky not to."

"If he has a history of scamming women

out of money, that would certainly be relevant."

"He has a history of scamming everybody out of everything."

"Well, I didn't get his rap sheet. But a check of vital statistics was rather interesting."

"Why, is he dead?"

"You'd be surprised how many times he's been married."

"I probably wouldn't."

"Eight. Four times since you. Most recently to a Miss Evelyn Anne Miller, an actress-slash-cocktail waitress considerably his junior."

"That would be Bambi. I met her."

"Oh?"

"He brought her to town. Just to throw in my face. In case his legal maneuvers weren't pissing me off enough. He was hoping a hot trophy wife might make me blow a gasket."

"Is it?"

"You haven't seen her. Jesus, Becky, she makes *you* look like Grandma Moses."

Becky pointed her finger. "Hey, watch it, or I'll charge you what I'm actually worth."

"In the meantime, I don't suppose you found out anything about that bank manager."

"What about him?"

"He seemed awfully eager to sell me down the river."

"Maybe."

"Chief Harper thinks it's funny. So do I. I was out at the guy's house just last week. Investigating an alleged burglary. In which nothing was taken, but a KenKen puzzle was left."

"What's a KenKen puzzle?"

"Oh, not again."

Cora went through the whole explanation about solving KenKen.

"What could it possibly mean?" Becky asked.

"I have no idea."

"Did you solve it?"

"Of course I solved it. It's a piece of cake."

"Let me see it."

Cora reached in her drawstring purse, found the KenKen.

Becky looked it over, said, "Hmmm."

"Hmmm? What do you mean, hmmm?"

"Well, one thing jumps out at you."

"What would that be?"

Becky pointed. "Look at the first line."

"What about it?"

"It's 1, 2, 4, 3."

"So? It's gotta be the numbers 1 through 4 in some order or another. There aren't that many possibilities."

"It's just interesting that it's that one."

"Why?"

"You didn't notice?" Becky smiled. "It's the amount of your alimony payment."

CHAPTER 17

Roger Randolph pulled into his driveway, stopped the car, and got out. He popped the trunk, took out the bag of groceries, and the case of light beer he'd picked up at the Stop & Shop, and went up the walk. Balancing the groceries and the beer with one arm, he fumbled with his keys and opened the front door. He went in, kicked the door shut behind him, shifted the weight of his burden, walked into the living room, and stopped dead.

Cora Felton was sitting on the couch. She was reading a mystery novel. She looked up when he came in. "About time you got home. I was beginning to worry."

"What are you doing in my house?"

"Reading a Joan Hess book." Cora held it up. "Quite funny, actually. You'd like it."

"How did you get in here?"

"Excellent question." Cora nodded in agreement with herself. "See, that's the question you should have been asking last Thursday. When the place was robbed and nothing was taken. How the hell did the robber get in? I guess you can't call him a robber if nothing was taken. And you can't call him a him or you'll get in trouble with the PC police. After all, the robber who wasn't a robber could well be a her. Like me, for instance."

"You broke into my house?"

"Not last Thursday. Last Thursday I came with Chief Harper. And, no, I wasn't coming back to the scene of the crime. That was the first time I'd ever been in your house. And this is not returning to the scene of the crime, either. Well, actually, it is, but not in the sense you mean it. Because I didn't *commit* the crime. You wanna put your beer down? It looks heavy."

Randolph set the beer and groceries on the floor, popped back up. "How dare you break into my house."

Cora pursed her lips. "Gee, I don't know. More chutzpah than the average bear? That's possible. Frustrated by the day in court? Another good one. Freaked out by meeting my accuser *before* my day in court? Before I was even summoned, for goodness sake? That's got to be pretty close to a winner."

"I don't know what you're talking about."

Cora shook her head. "Oh, no, no, no. How can you not know what I'm talking about? I was in your house, examining your quote robbery unquote, the one where nothing was taken and something was left. Now, surely you remember that."

"I'm going to call the police."

"Good. Ask for Dan Finley. He's waiting for my call."

"What?"

"You didn't think I'd come here without backup, did you? Well, actually, I would. I was bluffing about Dan Finley. But I've got a gun in my purse." Cora put up her hand. "Not to worry. I haven't shot anyone in ages. The point is I'm here, and I'd like to know what's going on."

"You're crazy. You're out of your mind."

Cora grimaced. "See, now, that's not the answer I was hoping for. Let me make it easier for you. Did you know my ex-husband before today?"

"No."

"That's Melvin. The one suing me now in court. Did you know him?"

"I said no."

"Okay. Did you know *of* him?"

"What?"

"Had you been contacted by anyone *rep-*

resenting Melvin? Had you been approached by anyone with any threats or inducements to do me wrong?"

"That's absurd."

"My sentiments exactly. Do you deny it?"

"Of course I deny it. Now will you get out of my house?"

"What did you think was stolen?"

"Huh?"

"When you called the police. To report the burglary. Where nothing was taken. What did you *think* was taken?"

"Nothing."

"Then why did you call the police?"

"My house was broken into. Maybe that doesn't mean anything to you. Obviously it doesn't, since you've just done it again."

"I haven't done it again. I never broke into your house before, and I resent the implication."

"This is a nightmare."

"Yes, but it's my nightmare, and I'm just trying to make it make sense. Let me put it this way. You meet any young blondes lately?"

"What?"

"Of the practically prepubescent variety. Sexy, alluring, and out of your league. Way too interested in you for your type of guy."

"Hey!"

"Anyone like that in your life?"

"My personal life is none of your business."

"Obviously not, or you'd be bragging about it. All right, let me put it another way. Do you do KenKen?"

"What?"

"The puzzle found in your safe. The Ken-Ken. Do you do them?"

"Why?"

"You *do.* That's interesting. Who knows you do KenKen? Is it a secret vice? Or do you do 'em on your coffee break at the bank? Or when things are just slow?"

"Would you leave? I gotta put my food away."

Cora heaved herself off the couch, grabbed a bag of groceries. "Come on. I'll help you." She headed for the kitchen.

Roger looked at her in exasperation. He picked up the case of beer, trailed along behind.

Cora put the bag of groceries on the kitchen table, opened the refrigerator door. "Here you go. Wanna put away the perishables? Maybe a couple of beers. I don't drink it, but you could probably use a few."

The banker still looked somewhat dazed. "This can't be happening."

"Yeah, but it is. What have we got here?

Milk. Orange juice. Healthy boy." She put the cartons in the fridge. "Got any eggs? Cottage cheese? Yogurt? Frozen foods? No, just cans and dry food. Looks like we're good to go."

Cora closed the refrigerator door. "So. This teller who brought you the check. Why did you remember it so vividly? She a cutie? You sweet on her?"

"I don't think I'm supposed to talk to you. Isn't there a law against tampering with witnesses?"

"Oh, for God's sake. This isn't a murder trial. This is a sneaky ploy by a scheming ex-husband in an alimony proceeding. Do you really want to be a part of that?"

"Now I am going to call the police."

"So the KenKen meant nothing to you."

"Of course not."

"Did you solve it?"

"Huh?"

"You do KenKen. Did you solve this one?"

"The police took it."

"Right. As evidence of the nonburglary. Well, I got good news for you." Cora reached into her floppy drawstring purse, pulled out a piece of paper. "I got a copy for you. Just in case you'd like to solve it."

"Why?"

"If someone broke into my house and left

110

something for me, I'd want to know what it was." Cora whipped out a pencil, thrust it at the banker. "Here you go. It's a 4-by-4. Piece of cake. Bet you can do it in less than a minute."

"I don't understand. Why do you want me to solve it?"

"Because it's there. You know, like why did they climb Everest. In this case, because it's there. In your room. After the robbery. I would think you'd like to know why." She cocked her head and said insinuatingly, "And if you *don't* want to know why, that would be interesting in itself."

The banker exhaled noisily. He snatched the pencil from her, solved the KenKen. Slapped the pencil down on the table. "There."

"That wasn't so hard, now, was it? Let's see if you got it right."

"Of course I got it right."

"I'm sure you did, but I'm going to take a look." Cora scanned the KenKen. "Yeah, that's it all right. That the first time you ever solved it?"

"Obviously."

"You had no idea what the answer was?"

"Not at all."

"Take a look at it, see if it means anything to you."

"How could it?"

"You tell me."

He glared at her, picked up the KenKen, scanned it, and put it back on the table.

"Well?" Cora said. "How about it? That ring any bells? Look familiar? Mean anything to you?"

He shook his head. "Not a damn thing."

CHAPTER 18

The phone rang in the middle of the night. Cora grabbed for it, knocked it off the nightstand. Or would have, had there *been* a phone on the nightstand. As it was, she knocked off her glasses, keys, and ashtray.

Cora heaved herself to her feet, stumbled past the other bedroom, where Sherry and Aaron were snoring like a pair of porpoises, worn out, no doubt, from connubial bliss. She staggered into the office, flipped on a light, grabbed the phone.

"Hello?" she growled.

"Cora?"

"Yes."

"Chief Harper."

"What the hell time is it?"

"Three A.M."

"This better be good."

"Randolph's dead."

"What?"

"He's been murdered. Shot in the head."

"It couldn't be self-inflicted?"

"No. It's murder."

"When was he killed?"

"I don't know."

Cora frowned. "How is that possible?"

"I gotta get off the phone. Just thought you'd like to know," Harper said, and hung up.

Cora described the chief in terms that were hardly laudatory yet loud and quite elaborate.

Sherry staggered in the door. "What's going on?"

"Harper called. It's a murder."

"Who?"

"Randolph."

"Guy who got robbed?"

"He wasn't really robbed."

"But he's really dead?"

"According to the chief."

Cora went back in her room and pulled on her clothes. Halfway through getting dressed, she stopped and checked her purse. Her gun was in it. It had not been fired.

Cora sighed.

That was a relief.

But only slightly.

It bothered her that she'd looked.

CHAPTER 19

There were three police cars out front. In the Bakerhaven police force, that constituted a quorum.

Officer Sam Brogan was stringing up crime scene ribbon with studied indifference. The cranky officer stroked his mustache, popped his gum.

"What have we got here, Sam?"

"We've got a murder in the middle of the night. Some people have no consideration."

"Don't take it personally."

"Oh, no? Were you happy getting the phone call?"

"Where's Dan?"

"Upstairs with the chief. We're still waiting on the doc."

The flashing lights of an ambulance came up the road. That wouldn't be the medical examiner, just an EMS team. They'd have to wait on the doctor as well.

Cora ducked under the crime scene ribbon.

"Sure, sure, just barge right in like I wasn't here," Sam said.

"The chief called me."

"Just bustin' your chops. Go on up."

"Where is it?"

"In the bedroom."

Cora went upstairs, looked in.

Randolph was in bed. It didn't take a medical examiner to tell he wasn't sleeping. He was lying diagonally with his feet on the pillow and his head at the foot of the bed. His eyes were wide open, staring. Blood drained from a wound in his temple.

Dan Finley was snapping pictures of the body from every conceivable angle. He waved hi and went on with his work.

Chief Harper came in from the bathroom. He'd just splashed water on his face, was wiping it with a towel. He grinned. "Well, you didn't waste any time."

"You called me."

"I didn't ask you to come here."

"You thought I wouldn't?"

"I knew you would. That's why I didn't ask you."

"Huh?"

"If I asked you down here, you'd figure I had a puzzle I wanted you to solve, and you

116

wouldn't want to do it. If I didn't ask you down here, you'd figure I didn't, and you'd want to. So I didn't and you did. You even beat the doc."

"It's three in the morning. I'm not sure what you just said. What have we got here?"

"Like I said on the phone. Gunshot wound to the head."

"And you know it wasn't self-inflicted because . . . ?"

"No gun. Kind of a dead giveaway. Suicides rarely dispose of the gun."

"You're making jokes, Chief?"

"Just anticipating yours. Someone shot him. I have no idea why. Or who. Or when. The only thing I know is where. Unless you think the body was dumped here."

Cora peered at the body. "From the amount of blood on the bed I would say you could rule that out. So you have no idea when."

"The body's cold. The beginning of rigor. The medical examiner can pin it down, but he's been dead a while."

"How's the body get found at three in the morning?"

"Actually, it was found at two. Neighbor got up to go to the bathroom. Saw the lights were on and the car in the driveway. David Harstein. Nosy old coot. Has a reputation for butting into other people's business. Knew Randolph wouldn't be up at that hour. Figured something was wrong."

"And?"

"Called the cops."

"And?"

Harper made a face. "Sam was on duty. By the time he got through bawling David out for waking him up on a damn fool errand —"

"Sam wasn't asleep," Dan put in. "He was wide awake, ever vigilant."

"Right. Anyway, Sam took a ride over, found the front door open, went in."

"The neighbor a suspect?"

"I can't imagine. I suppose stranger things have happened."

"Why the hell would anyone want to kill the banker?"

"He testified against you yesterday, didn't he."

"Right. And then made me so angry I came over here and killed him."

"You *do* get angry."

"My gun's in my purse. Wanna check it? I didn't kill him, Chief."

"I'm sure you didn't. If I check your purse, I'll be able to attest to that fact."

"I could have used another gun."

"Cora."

"I got one gun in my purse. Mine. Fully loaded. Hasn't been fired. Here. Take a look."

Harper gave the gun a cursory look. He didn't even bother to sniff the barrel.

Cora stuck it back in her purse.

There were footsteps on the stairs, and Barney Nathan came in. Even at three in the morning he wore a bow tie. Cora wondered if it was a clip-on.

"Okay. Let's pronounce him and get him out of here."

A EMS team had followed the doctor up the stairs and were waiting in the doorway. Largely for their benefit, the doctor made a show of feeling for a pulse. "Okay, he's dead. Probably a good twelve hours. And if it wasn't from that bullet wound to the head, I'd be very much surprised. All right, guys, take him away."

As the EMS team loaded the body onto a gurney, Cora noticed one of them was a woman. She sighed, said, "Aw, hell."

Harper said, "What?"

Cora jerked her thumb. "Girl on the gurney. Isn't very big. As she's loading him up, I'm wondering if she could carry the banker. Which is sexist. I'm thinking I was a lot happier before political correctness made me be so goddamned careful."

119

"You really want to be politically correct, you probably shouldn't call her a girl."

"Oh, for chrissakes. Okay, Chief. You lured, tricked, enticed me into coming out here. For no conceivable reason that I can think of. You wanna tell me what's up?"

"Only if you don't get mad."

"Why would I get mad?"

"I don't know why you do half the things you do."

"Chief."

"It's late. I didn't want to get into everything on the phone."

"Everything?"

"Every little detail. After all, you just woke up."

"Chief, I'm going to strangle you in a moment. What are you holding back?"

"There was something on the bed beside the body."

"Don't tell me."

"Okay."

Cora's face flushed. "Damn it, that's a figure of speech. What did you find?"

Dan Finley's evidence kit was on the floor. Chief Harper reached inside, pulled out a plastic evidence bag. There was a piece of paper in it. He held it up for Cora to see.

It was a KenKen.

15+			4x		2-
	1-	3÷		5-	
4-			11+		1-
	2÷	7+		1-	
14+			11+		6+

CHAPTER 20

Cora was hopelessly conflicted. The Ken-Ken was a good news/bad news scenario. The good news was it wasn't a crossword puzzle she couldn't solve, it was a number puzzle she could. The bad news was it was any puzzle at all. Because Chief Harper would want to connect it with the crime, and Cora knew damn well there wasn't any way it would.

"So?" Harper said.

"So what?"

"Can you help me out?"

"I sure can. With some sound advice. Ignore this number puzzle and figure out who committed the crime."

"That's not what I mean, and you know it."

"Yeah, but it's the best advice I've got. Come on, Chief, you want me to solve this thing? I'll tell you what it is. It's a 6-by-6 KenKen. Which is similar to a 4-by-4 Ken-

Ken, only bigger. It will have the numbers 1 through 6, and the mathematical functions still apply. You want me to solve it, I can, but it will take a little more time than a 4-by-4."

"How much time?"

"Two to three weeks."

"What!"

"That's a slight exaggeration. I could do it right now, except it's evidence, and you don't want me to write on the paper. Fax me a copy when you get around to it."

"That won't be until tomorrow."

"Oh, my God! How awful! Someone might get some sleep first. Come on, Chief, when I solve this you know what you're gonna get? Thirty-six numbers. Six of them will be 1's, six of them will be 2's. And this guy will still be dead, and you won't know any more than you did before unless you get some other lead. So. Can I have the puzzle? I'll solve it for you right now."

"No."

"That's what I thought. In that case, I'm going home. Let me know if you come up with anything."

Cora smiled and went downstairs.

Sam Brogan was standing guard or doing a great impression of a cow sleeping on its feet. Cora couldn't tell which without snapping her fingers in his face, which seemed rude. She murmured, "Good night, Sam," didn't wait for a reply, ducked under the crime scene ribbon, got in her car, and drove off.

Her hands were shaking.

What had she done? She'd withheld the fact that she'd called on the banker that very afternoon. She'd had every opportunity to mention it, and she hadn't. Why? Why didn't she tell Chief Harper? Because Dan Finley was there? That was a convenient excuse. You wouldn't wanna spill your guts in front of a witness. But why not? It wasn't as if she had anything to hide. She had nothing to do with the man's death, and nothing she had to say could possibly incriminate her. She was absolutely, one hundred percent in the clear.

Except now.

Now that she'd left the scene of the crime, she was guilty of holding out on the police. That technically made her guilty of compounding a felony and conspiring to conceal a crime.

That was ridiculous. She wasn't concealing a crime. The crime was murder, and it wasn't concealed at all. Everyone knew about it. Paying a social call on the banker was not a crime, and failing to mention that

124

fact, the fact that had absolutely nothing to do with the murder, could not possibly be construed as obstruction of justice.

Could it?

Cora considered calling Becky Baldwin. She wondered how the young lawyer would feel about being rousted out of bed in the dead of night. She'd probably be okay with it if Cora were a suspect offering a retainer. But Cora wasn't a suspect. She was an innocent bystander, whose only mistake had been marrying the wrong man some umpteen years ago, an indiscretion for which she seemed destined to never cease being punished.

As far as Cora was concerned, the death of this banker was just one in a series of nasty manipulations engineered by Melvin in order to wreck her day.

Cora pulled up the driveway. The new addition flickered in the headlights like some huge monster lying in wait. Cora switched off the lights, went up the walk.

Sherry met her at the front door.

"What are you doing up?"

"I couldn't sleep."

"Where's Aaron?"

"He could."

"A murder, and your newspaper reporter hubby couldn't care?"

"The *Gazette*'s a morning paper, and it's already off the press. He figures there's no point losing sleep for a story that won't run for over twenty-four hours."

"Good God. Was he that jaded before he got married?"

"He's not jaded. Just tired."

"Aren't you tired?"

"Couldn't sleep."

"You nauseous?"

"No, I am not *nauseated.* You need to practice your grammar."

"Not at three in the morning, I don't. You were puking your guts out? That's why you're up?"

"I'm up because the guy who testified against you yesterday is dead. I wanted to be ready to go in case I had to post bail."

"I had nothing to do with the man's death."

"Right. And innocent people are never accused."

"You think Chief Harper would arrest me?"

"He has before."

"Yeah, but he had cause. This time I haven't done anything."

"Then why are you nervous?"

"What?"

"You're irritable. Jumpy."

"It's three in the morning."

"Even so. I know you. What did you do now?"

Cora took a breath. "I held out on the cops."

"What?"

Cora told Sherry about calling on the banker.

"Go back. Go back and tell him what you just told me."

"It's too late. I already withheld it."

"You didn't withhold it. You just didn't mention it. In the heat of the moment. With so many things on your mind."

"Yeah. And if you believe that one . . ."

"You don't want my advice? So call Becky Baldwin."

"I don't think she'd be happy to hear from me."

"So what?"

"I'll call her tomorrow." Cora flopped down on the couch. "Really, now. Why are you up? And don't give me that about bail."

"I thought you might need me."

"Oh?"

"There wasn't a crossword puzzle with the body?"

"No. There was a KenKen."

"Really. Did you solve it?"

"I can't solve it till they give me a copy."

"Why didn't they?"

"Kind of a low priority. Just a bunch of numbers."

"You think it means anything?"

"No."

"Then why was it there?"

Cora grimaced. "See, that's the whole problem. That's what I always get stuck with. 'You're the Puzzle Lady, here's a puzzle, somebody must have left it for you.' What rubbish."

"Why is that rubbish?"

"It's ridiculous."

"It happens."

"It happened once. Now every time there's a murder that's what they expect."

"It happened more than once."

"Bite your tongue. It's never happened with a KenKen. A KenKen is a number puzzle. It can't possibly mean a thing."

"It happened with a sudoku."

"And the sudoku had a crossword puzzle attached to point me in the right direction."

"Actually . . ."

"Actually?" Cora looked at her niece suspiciously. "Did you just say actually?"

"When you were zooming out of here I noticed the flag on the mailbox was up."

"In the dark?"

"In the headlights."

"So Aaron was mailing a letter."

"Aaron wasn't mailing a letter."

"You woke him up and asked him?"

"Aaron doesn't mail letters. Not from here. Anything he sends goes out from the paper."

"That's a hell of a marriage. Aren't you afraid he's writing his mistress?"

"Aaron doesn't *have* a mistress. You can't judge all marriages by your own disasters."

"Disasters?"

"Would you consider Melvin a crowning achievement?"

"Point taken. What about the mailbox?"

"I found this." Sherry whipped out an envelope. Written on the front were the words PUZZLE LADY. "Guess what was in it?"

"You opened my letter?"

"It's a fine line. On the one hand, you're the Puzzle Lady. On the other hand, I do the work. And I open all the checks and bills."

"Yeah, yeah, fine. What's in it?"

Sherry passed it over.

Cora took the envelope, pulled out the paper.

It was a crossword puzzle.

ACROSS

1 Where Pago Pago is
6 Island north of New Zealand
10 "Little Women" character
14 Vote into office
15 Knot-tying vows
16 K-12, in education

17 Big artery
18 Message, part 1
20 With 47-Across, where to look
22 Come before
23 Juror, in theory
25 Chow down
26 Message, part 2
30 Predicaments
34 Expert
35 Insecticide brand
36 Family name in baseball
37 Novocaine-treated
39 Accumulate
42 Use a teething ring
43 Sheltered, at sea
44 Barbershop spinner
46 Auction call
47 See 20-Across
48 Message, part 3
51 "_____ Can Cook" (PBS show)
52 Story starter
53 Outdoors, to a diner
58 Become dotty
62 Message, part 4
64 Austerity
65 Tied, as a score
66 Conclusion lead-in
67 Baseball manager Joe
68 Benefit of clergy, e.g.

69 Kind of terrier
70 Flips out

DOWN

1   Wet septet
2   _____ vera
3   Certain Ford, for short
4   Squid relatives
5   Finished
6   Little white lie
7   Light bulb, in cartoons
8   Group seeker
9   Does not attend
10 Bit of sweat
11 Exile site of 1814
12 One of those things?
13 Make yourself scarce
19 Go fetch
21 Bing Crosby's record label
24 Hotel unit
26 Tired and trite
27 Eyes
28 Mocha setting
29 Not fitting
30 Boxer's punch
31 Accused's excuse
32 Design idea
33 Blue shoe material?
38 Buzzer

40 Area near TriBeCa
41 Broken arm holder
45 Keeps company (with)
48 Converts to bills?
49 Pop open, as champagne
50 Military unit
51 "Fine with me!"
53 Say it's so
54 Clothier Strauss
55 Sweat it out
56 Chicago Cubs star Sandberg
57 Bacchanal
59 Taj Mahal town
60 Trail mix
61 Mars, to the Greeks
63 Time keeper, at times

CHAPTER 21

Cora cocked her head and laid into her niece with elaborate sarcasm. "So. Staying up to go my bail. That was the first lie. The second lie, closer to the truth, was staying up *in case* there was a crossword puzzle. Gee, what were the odds of that? When you had it right in your hand."

"I didn't want to bring it up until you told me your end of the story."

"Why not?"

"Because I knew you'd react like this, and I'd never find out what happened."

"Sherry, this is no good. You got married, and you're getting devious. That's to be expected. But you're supposed to get devious with your husband. That's who you need to trick. Not your loyal, trusting aunt."

"You're going through an alimony hearing, so I can forgive your views on marriage."

"Oh, bite me! What does the crossword puzzle mean? Why didn't you solve it?"

"I solved it. I duped it in the fax machine and solved the copy. You wanna see?"

"Well, I'm sure not going to solve it myself."

Sherry took out the solved copy, passed it over. "See, I didn't think it meant anything until you told me about the KenKen. You throw that into the mix."

"What mix? What does it say?"

Cora looked the puzzle over.

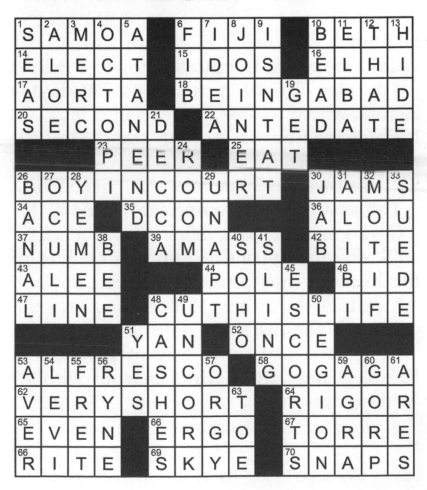

Cora read the theme entry. " 'Being a bad boy in court cut his life very short.' Great. The guy testifies against me and gets whacked. Is this saying I did it?"

"I don't think so."

"Well, what else could it mean?"

"Don't forget the KenKen."

"What about the KenKen? This doesn't have anything to do with the KenKen."

"No. But look at 20 Across."

"Huh?"

"Look."

Cora looked at the puzzle.

The clue for 20 Across was "With 47-Across, where to look."

The clue for 47 Across was "See 20-Across."

The answer to 20 Across was "Second."

The answer to 47 Across was "Line."

Cora groaned. "Oh, hell."

"See?" Sherry said. "The second line of the KenKen must mean something."

"Yeah."

"What's the matter?"

"I gotta figure some way of getting the KenKen away from Chief Harper without seeming too eager."

CHAPTER 22

Becky was pissed.

"You didn't call me?"

"At three in the morning?"

"It wasn't to borrow a cup of sugar, it was a murder."

"I'm not a suspect."

"So what?"

"What would you have done?"

"Try to figure out who *was* a suspect, and lock that person up with a retainer."

"Well, you go, girl. Harper hasn't charged anyone yet, so no harm, no foul."

Becky looked at Cora thoughtfully. "Why are you here?"

"Huh?"

"If you're not involved in the case, why are you up so early? You were running around at three in the morning. I'd think you'd need your sleep."

"Are you saying I look tired?" Cora said acidly.

"I would say you seem mendacious."

Uh-oh. Mendacious. Just the type of word Cora was always on the alert for, the type of word a crossword puzzle person should know that would give her away if she didn't.

Cora dug into her extensive motion picture knowledge and came up with the scene in *Cat on a Hot Tin Roof* where Burl Ives is talking to Paul Newman about the odor of mendacity in the house.

"Are you calling me a liar?"

"I'm wondering why you're taking such an interest in this case."

"He was a witness. He testified against me."

"And now he won't. Problem solved."

"Becky."

"You didn't kill the guy, by any chance?"

"Of course not."

"Then I don't see the problem. Come on, Cora, what do you want?"

"Aw, hell."

Cora told Becky about withholding the fact that she'd called on the victim.

"That's not exactly good."

"No."

"If it came out, you might get charged with something minor. I could defend you, rack up a nice fee."

"Becky."

"And that's the worst-case scenario."

"It didn't sound worse from your point of view."

"That's the shyster in me talking. Just ignore it. So?"

"So. There was a KenKen next to the body."

"What about it?"

"I'd like to get a hold of it."

"Won't Chief Harper want you to solve it?"

"Yeah, but he's in no rush."

"And you are?"

"I'd like to see it."

"So ask him."

"I don't want to appear too eager."

"Would you like me to?"

"That wouldn't be good, either."

"What do you want me to do?"

"That's a tough one. Best-case scenario, I'd like you to represent Melvin, take a dive, and have him found guilty of murder."

"Does anyone suspect him of murder?"

"That's the problem."

"I see. What's the second-best-case scenario?"

"I'd like the murder to turn out to have nothing to do with me."

"What are the odds of that?"

"With a damn KenKen? What do you think?"

"I take it Chief Harper doesn't know about the other KenKen."

"What about it?"

"It being the amount of your alimony check."

"That's arbitrary, extraneous, and most likely a coincidence."

"So he doesn't know?"

"Of course he doesn't know. If he did, I'd be in custody now, and you'd be trying to get me out."

"That sounds good. That's the type of thing a lawyer can deal with."

"I'm glad you like it. If Harper gets an anonymous tip, I'll know who to blame."

"I'm not turning you in. I'm just saying, if Harper knew about the solution of the first KenKen, he'd be more interested in the second."

"It's a good thing he doesn't."

"But you're interested in the second, and you want to see the puzzle."

"That's right."

"Any particular reason?"

Cora hesitated. Becky was her lawyer. There was no reason not to tell her about the crossword puzzle. On the other hand, there was no reason to tell her *now*. Of course, that would make her more of a principal player, which would whet Becky's interest. But in practical terms, that energy would more likely be expended extracting a fee.

Becky was pissing her off. Cora was tired of being a punching bag.

"I'll let you know."

CHAPTER 23

For a man with a murder, Chief Harper didn't seem particularly concerned. He tipped back in his desk chair, sipped his coffee, nibbled on a scone from Cushman's Bake Shop. "Well, Barney Nathan kicked in with the autopsy. At least the preliminary report. It seems the guy was killed in the early evening. Most likely between six and eight." Harper took another sip of coffee. "Not that I'd hold him to it, if I could find someone did it at five forty-five."

"What have you found?" Cora said impatiently.

"Well, I haven't found the killer, if that's what you mean."

"Why not?"

"Come on, Cora, the case just broke. Usually I got twenty-four hours before the media accuses me of dragging my feet."

"I'm not asking if you solved the damn thing, I'm just asking what you know."

"Why are you so interested?"

"It's not every day a complaining witness against me gets taken out."

"Are you saying that's the motive?"

"I certainly hope not. If someone starts bumping off witnesses, it would make for an awful long hearing." Harper looked at her. "Come on, Chief. You wouldn't be sitting there calmly eating scones unless you had something. What have you got?"

"I've got nothing official."

"And unofficially?"

"I've got gossip, rumors, and innuendo."

Cora rubbed her hands together. "Ooo, that's the stuff. Come on, let's have it."

"You understand none of this is to go any further."

"Of course not."

"Particularly to any nephews-in-law who might be living in your house." He frowned. "Is that an actual relationship? Nephew-in-law? Or do I have to say the guy who married your niece?"

"I don't care what you say, I won't tell him. What have you got?"

"Not much. Guy didn't seem to have any friends. Got an aging mother in Iowa somewhere, deciding if we should ship the body back to her. As far as the town goes, he's been here two years. Came here from Danbury, where he also worked in a bank. Transferred in as an opportunity for advancement, accepted a promotion. His co-workers express the usual shock and awe, but you get the impression none of the tellers liked him very much. Of course, he had two strikes against him, transferring in over their heads. Still, you'd hardly expect them to take him out."

"You're being awfully flippant about this, Chief. Why is that? Is it because you happen to know who did it?"

"No, it's because I have absolutely no idea. Dan Finley processed the crime scene for fingerprints, couldn't find a damn one. Not even the victim's. The gun had been taken. There was nothing at the crime scene except that puzzle, and yes, you can get fingerprints from paper, and no, there weren't any. The only thing we got is the puzzle."

"Then why aren't you banging down my door to solve it?"

"I figure you need your sleep. You were up all night."

"So were you."

"Yeah, but that's my job. I gotta stay up when there's nothing to do. I gotta speak to the media when there's nothing to say. I gotta put a good spin on everything when there's nothing to spin. I've already had a call from Channel Eight. They'd like an interview as soon as possible."

"What are you going to tell them?"

"I thought I'd lead off with the fact the guy's dead. You always like to get the main idea across."

"Chief."

"I got nothing, Cora. I don't know where to begin."

Cora took a breath. "The guy was in court yesterday."

"Testifying against you."

"Right. But since I didn't kill him, how about trying another angle? He testified for my rat bastard ex Melvin. That should put him near the top of the heap."

"He testified *for* Melvin."

"Yeah, but suppose he was going to back out?"

"Back out on what? The fact you cashed the check?"

"We don't know the facts, Chief."

"Never mind the facts. We don't even have a conjecture. You want to suggest any way I could tell the media your ex-husband's involved?"

"How about his lawyer? I wouldn't trust that guy any further than I can throw him."

"One problem. What's the motive?"

145

"You don't have a motive. It's early in the investigation. You're running down leads."

"That's not leads. That's wishful thinking."

"You're not tracing the gun?"

"No. At least we know what type we're looking for. It's a .45-caliber slug the doc took out of his brain." Harper cocked his head. "So. Wanna solve the KenKen?"

"Thought you'd never ask."

4	3	5	1	2	6
3	5	6	2	1	4
1	4	2	5	6	3
5	1	3	6	4	2
6	2	4	3	5	1
2	6	1	4	3	5

Cora whipped through the puzzle. She looked at the second line of the solution. It meant absolutely nothing to her. She tried to keep the relief out of her voice, said casually, "Can I have a copy?"

"Why?"

"Because it doesn't mean anything to me now. Maybe something will come to mind."

"You think it will?"

"Frankly, no. But I'd feel like a damn fool if something occurred to me later tonight and I didn't have a copy to check."

"Dan!"

Dan Finley stuck his head in the door. "Yeah, Chief."

"Run Cora off a copy, will you?"

"It mean anything?"

"No."

"Then why do you want one?"

"So I don't have to keep explaining why I don't have one," Cora said in exasperation.

"Come on, Dan, don't give Cora a hard time."

"Sorry. I've had Rick Reed on the phone four times this morning, looking for a lead. You gonna give him an interview?"

"I have to, but I got nothing to say."

"Don't worry," Cora said. "It's Rick. Smile, say 'alleged,' tell him you can't confirm. The interview will be over before he figures out what."

"Very funny. That's not going to work."

"Okay, try this. Pick Melvin up, ask him if he was hiding in the back of the courtroom listening to the testimony."

"Was he?"

"He sure was."

"Well, so what?"

Cora smiled. "That's the alleged thing you can't confirm. The fact that Melvin was spying on the guy's court testimony the same day he was killed. You have absolutely no comment."

"Why would Rick Reed think to ask me that?"

"Pick Melvin up and ask him."

CHAPTER 24

Melvin was surprised to find the police chief knocking on his door. "You looking for me?"

"That's right."

"What about?"

"Were you in court yesterday?"

"Why?"

Harper frowned. "These questions are preliminary and will go a lot faster if you cooperate. Let me help you out. You're suing your ex-wife to reduce your alimony. Your lawyer was in court, you weren't with him, but I have reason to believe you were watching from the back. Does that jog your memory?"

"Once again, I would like to know why."

"A witness at that hearing was killed last night. We're investigating a homicide, and I would appreciate some cooperation."

Melvin's face remained neutral; he was a good poker player, giving nothing away. "A witness, you say?"

"That's right. The banker."

"I see."

"That doesn't bother you?"

"I didn't know the man."

"Won't his death affect your court case?"

"I fail to see why. There's nothing he testified to that can't be corroborated by other sources."

"Then you were in court yesterday?"

"Did I say that?"

"Are you saying you weren't?"

"I don't recall saying anything."

"That's the problem. I told you, it's a murder investigation. We like it when people cooperate."

"I'm sure you do. It would be really awful if someone with valuable information failed to help. I'm sorry I don't have any. But I never met the man in question. I can't imagine who would want him dead."

"You can't help me?"

"You might want to ask my lawyer."

"You have the right to an attorney."

"I'm glad to hear it. But I don't need one. I'm just pointing out my attorney probably talked to the guy. You'd have to ask him yourself. I certainly don't want to speak for him."

A young blonde came out the door, managed to insinuate herself under Melvin's arm. She was wearing a blue tank top and white shorts. A pair of sunglasses were perched on her head. She might have been on her way to the beach. "You under arrest, honey?"

"Not so far." Melvin cocked his head at the chief. "You weren't hauling me in, were you? Despite that feeble excuse for a Miranda warning."

"And who might this be?"

"I'm Bambi. He was with me, and he didn't do it." She crinkled her nose. "What is it he didn't do?"

"Murder the banker who testified at his alimony hearing."

Bambi wasn't nearly as good a poker player as Melvin. The news jogged her out of her complacency. "What?"

"Roger Randolph was found shot to death in his home last night. I was hoping Mr. Crabtree could help us out. But he seems unusually noncommittal."

Bambi recovered her composure. She smiled at Melvin. "Honey, did you kill someone and not tell me?"

"I always tell you when I kill someone, sweetie. I swear, I haven't killed anyone in weeks."

"You guys are staying here for a while?"

"It's hard to say. There's this legal proceeding."

"It's not that hard to say." Harper looked from one to the other. "Don't leave town."

CHAPTER 25

Rick Reed was at his inquisitive best. The on-camera reporter cocked his head and favored Chief Harper with a knowing glance. "Well, now, Chief, you say you have no suspects at the present time. But is it or is it not a fact that you've questioned people in this affair?"

"That goes without saying."

"Well, then, let's say it," Rick announced triumphantly, as if he had proved a point. "The police have questioned people in this matter."

"That's our job."

"And who have you questioned?"

"Everyone who knew the decedent. Everyone who had business with the decedent. Everyone who had come in contact with the decedent within the last forty-eight hours."

"And who might that be?"

"Actually, quite a number. The decedent worked in a bank. He was observed there by all his co-workers."

"Was he seen by anyone else?"

"He was seen by the killer."

"Then the killer is not a co-worker."

"That's your deduction, not mine."

"Are you saying the killer could have been a co-worker?"

"At this point, nothing is ruled out."

"I understand the decedent was in court."

"That's right."

"Is it true that he testified against Baker-haven's own Puzzle Lady?"

"I wouldn't say he testified against her."

"He testified in the matter regarding her alimony?"

"That's right."

"Her ex-husband was seeking to have it stopped?"

"Yes."

"And he was called by her ex-husband?"

"By his lawyer, yes."

"Then he testified against her."

"You're free to draw that conclusion. I'm just telling you what happened."

"Did you question the Puzzle Lady about the murder?"

"I discussed it with her."

"What about her ex-husband? Have you questioned him?"

"As a matter of fact, I have."

"What did you question him about?"

"Whether he was in court when the decedent testified."

"Why wouldn't he be?"

"I have no idea. Apparently he wasn't at the plaintiff's table with his lawyer. I asked him if he was watching from the back of the courtroom."

"What did he say?"

"He didn't answer the question."

Rick Reed was astonished. "But you're a police officer."

"So they tell me," Harper said dryly.

"He refused to answer a direct question from a police officer in a murder investigation?"

"He wasn't picked up as a suspect, so he was under no obligation to."

"Well, what about his civic duty?"

"You'd have to ask him."

"What about the rest of your investigation?"

"Everyone is cooperating fully. We hope to have something soon."

Rick Reed turned to the camera. "Well. What an astounding turn of events. A key witness in a murder investigation refusing to answer questions for the police. A tactic usually reserved for the defendant. Yet, according to Police Chief Dale Harper, this man is not under arrest. This is Rick Reed, Channel Eight News."

Cora picked up the zapper, froze the image on the new TV set. "God, I love high-definition. Look how Rick Reed's face blends just the right amount of studied arrogance and naïve credulity."

Aaron sawed off a piece of pork roast, sopped it in sauce. "You realize there's not a damn thing in that interview I could get away with printing in the paper."

"That's Rick Reed for you," Sherry said. "A totally vapid interview, full of sound and fury, signifying nothing."

"Sound and fury?" Cora said skeptically.

"All right, sound *bites* and fury."

"I'm not happy with fury."

"Sound bites and *flurry?*"

"We're still not there."

"Kids, kids," Aaron said. "Sort out the linguistics later. What's this about Melvin?"

"I don't know," Cora said innocently.

"Right. Like you've got nothing to do with it."

"I may have given Chief Harper a hint."

"What's the idea?"

"Well, the guy's running around here with a blond nymphet. Why should he get off scot-free?"

"You think he killed the banker?"

"No, but I find it very suspicious the banker dies before I'm able to demonstrate my innocence."

"Innocence?" Sherry said. "Oh, for goodness' sakes."

"What's wrong with that?"

"Well, the banker said that you deposited a check. You *did* deposit a check. Left to you by your dear, departed husband, whom you never met. You mind telling me how you establish your innocence for that?"

Cora looked at Aaron. "She's very cranky today. You noticed these violent mood swings lately?"

"I'm going to kill you," Sherry said.

"Like that, for instance."

"She's trying to change the subject, Aaron. Ask her whether or not she had a hand in framing her ex-husband for murder."

Cora waved her hand. "Oh, pooh. No one had a hand in framing anyone for anything. It's the beginning of a murder investigation. Nothing is known, so you gotta stir things up."

"Nothing is known?" Aaron said.

"That's right."

"I thought a puzzle was found at the scene of the crime."

"A KenKen. That's right. And I solved it,

and it means absolutely nothing. Take a look."

Cora pulled the copy out of her drawstring purse, passed it over.

Aaron grabbed it before Sherry could.

"Hey! You didn't do that *before* we were married."

"Sorry. You go first."

"Okay. Now, you put this together with the crossword."

"Crossword!" Aaron said. "What crossword?"

"Oh," Cora said. "Is your wife holding out on you? That's never a good sign."

"There was a crossword?"

"Don't ask me," Cora said, putting up her hands. "I'm not the crossword person. I'm just the pretty face."

"Sherry?"

Sherry grimaced. "There's a clue, and you can't write it. Would you like to know what it is?"

"I'm your husband."

"Good. Get in husband mode and out of reporter mode and I'll show you the crossword."

"What crossword? What are you talking about?"

"Go get it, Sherry. I'll fill him in."

Cora told Aaron what happened while

Sherry retrieved the crossword.

Aaron picked up the puzzle, looked it over. " 'Being a bad boy in court cut his life very short?' That points to you."

"Thanks for your help," Cora said. "I never could have figured that out."

"So, what does it mean?"

"Seeing as how I didn't kill him, I haven't a clue."

"What about the KenKen numbers? Are they any help?"

"Not really. According to the crossword puzzle, the answers to 20 and 47 Across tell you where to look. The answers are 'second line.' If that means the second line of the KenKen, it's 3, 5, 6, 2, 1, 4. Which is not particularly helpful."

"Suppose the numbers aren't numbers," Aaron said.

Sherry frowned. "How could that be?"

"Easy. They stand for letters of the alphabet."

"Pretty short alphabet. You've got only six numbers. A, B, C, D, E, F."

"So?" Aaron said. "Maybe that's all you need. Let's see what we've got. The numbers are 3, 5, 6, 2, 1, 4. That's C-E-F-B-A-D."

"Cefbad?" Sherry said. "That's not particularly illuminating."

" 'Bad' sounds like Melvin," Cora pointed out.

"Yeah. And what's 'cef'?"

"That's a little harder," she admitted. "I suppose they could be the notes of a scale. As long as you don't have a ti."

"What?" Aaron said.

"You've got do, re, me, fa, sol, la. You don't have ti."

"We have coffee," Aaron said.

"Hit him for me, Sherry. Come on, what if they're notes of a scale. Then 3 would be me, 5 would be sol, 6 would be la, 2 would be re, 1 would be do, and 4 would be fa. So we've got me-sol —"

"Isn't that a soup?" Aaron suggested.

"You're not helping," Sherry said.

"And we've got la-re-do."

"The town! It's a soup in a town!"

"Sherry, you married a wise-ass punk and I'm going to kill him."

"What's the last one?"

"Fa." Cora looked at Aaron. "Because it's too fa to go to la-re-do to get your soup."

"Okay," Sherry said. "If it's not the first six letters of the alphabet and it's not musical notes, what have we got?"

"Have we ruled out the 'numbers are numbers' theory?" Aaron said.

"Six numbers. It's too short for a telephone number. Too short for a Social Security number."

"Suppose it's a lottery number?" Cora suggested.

"Oh, that's helpful."

"Hey, if this number wins, don't blame me."

"Could it be a license plate number?" Aaron said.

"They're letters and numbers."

"There you go. Maybe it's a license plate."

"Sure, if the license plate doesn't have any letters beyond F. When you try to represent twenty-six letters with six numbers, it just doesn't work."

"Suppose you got more," Aaron said. "We've got 356214. Say 21 is not BA, it's the twenty-first letter of the alphabet."

"Which is?"

"It's U."

"You think it's me?"

"I think it's the letter *U.* That's the twenty-first letter of the alphabet."

"Okay," Cora said. "Then, taking them two at a time, what is the *thirty-fifth* letter of the alphabet?"

"Okay, let's compromise," Aaron said.

"What do you mean?"

"How about something that uses *more* of the letters of the alphabet."

"All of them?"

"No, but maybe enough. Six isn't good. What if we use three times that."

Cora frowned. "What do you mean?"

Aaron took out his cell phone, flipped it open. "It's a text message. 2 is A, B, C. 3 is D, E, F."

"I see what you mean," Cora said. "So, what have we got here?"

"Well, let's see. 356214. 3 is DEF. 5 is JKL. 6 is MNO."

"What about the 1? It doesn't stand for any letters."

"1 is 1. This could be a combination of numbers and letters. If it's a license plate number, it probably is. A lot of license plate numbers, the first digits are letters, and the last three are numbers."

"Oh, really," Cora said. "Those last three numbers are 214."

"So?"

"Those happen to be the numbers of *my* license plate."

"Oh, yeah. What's the rest of it?"

"Electric Light Orchestra."

"Huh?"

"ELO."

"Let's see. 3 could be E. 5 could be L. 6 could be O. There you are. ELO214."

Aaron looked up at Cora. "Looks like you did it."

CHAPTER 26

Judge Hobbs surveyed the crowded court-room with distaste. "It is somewhat unusual to have so many spectators at a simple alimony hearing. I understand how the circumstances of the past forty-eight hours have created interest in this matter. However, those circumstances have absolutely no bearing in this case, and are not to be raised. If that is why you are here, you are bound to be disappointed. So, when you find out this is not what you hoped to see, I would ask you to please leave quietly and not disturb the proceedings.

"Now then. When we adjourned, the plaintiff was putting on his case."

Becky was on her feet. "Actually, the plaintiff was doing nothing of the sort. The plaintiff isn't even here. The plaintiff's *lawyer* was putting on his case, but I don't see his client."

"Mr. Fleckstein, do you intend to proceed

in the absence of your client?"

"No, I do not, Your Honor. In fact, here he is now."

All heads turned as Melvin made a star's entrance through the back door of the courtroom and strode down the aisle. Every eye was on the charismatic figure. Even Cora was impressed. The man still had it. Smug, arrogant, self-assured, Melvin was at his scene-stealing best. He pushed open the gate, walked through, and sat down next to his attorney.

"Mr. Crabtree," Judge Hobbs said. "Nice of you to grace us with your presence."

"My pleasure, Your Honor. But if we could move things along, I need to get back to work. I happen to be supporting several ex-wives."

A ripple of amusement, largely female, swept through the courtroom.

Judge Hobbs banged the gavel. "Mr. Crabtree. In the future, if you wish to address the court, please do so through your attorney. Mr. Fleckstein, call your next witness."

Before he could, Becky Baldwin rose to her feet. "One moment, Your Honor. I think you may have lost track of the fact that court was adjourned before I had an opportunity to cross-examine Mr. Randolph."

"You were certainly given that opportunity."

"I don't believe I was. He completed his direct examination, you asked me if I had anything to refute it, I asked for an adjournment, and you granted one. I don't recall being offered the opportunity to cross-examine, and I don't recall saying, 'No questions.' Before Mr. Fleckstein calls another witness, I would like the opportunity to cross-examine his last one."

"Oh, Your Honor —"

Judge Hobbs banged the gavel. "That will do, Mr. Fleckstein. I'll handle this. Ms. Baldwin, obviously you cannot cross-examine the last witness, as you well know. But your claim that you were not given an opportunity to do so is tenuous at best. I think a look at the transcript will prove that is not correct."

"I doubt that, Your Honor. I ordered a copy of the transcript and went over it quite carefully. Clearly, I was never asked to cross-examine."

"That might well be, Ms. Baldwin. But the point would seem somewhat moot."

"Not at all, Your Honor. The witness gave direct examination. If I am not allowed to cross-examine, it stands uncontested. Which, of course, it cannot be. I therefore move the witness's entire direct examination be stricken from the record."

Fleckstein erupted from his chair, spouting objections.

Melvin, however, was calm. He glanced over at the defense table with a bemused look on his face and grinned roguishly at Becky Baldwin with newfound interest.

CHAPTER 27

"Watch yourself," Cora warned. Court was in recess, and she and Becky were holed up in one of the conference rooms.

"What do you mean?"

"Melvin thinks you're hot."

"You're kidding."

"Not at all. I've seen that look before."

"Cora."

"He likes the way you're beating up his attorney. He thinks you've got spunk. You do. Don't let him flatter you."

"Don't worry about it."

"I worry about everything where Melvin's concerned. I can worry about me. I can worry about you. The nymphet's not in court, so he's running his game. He's always running his game. If he tries to speak to you, be careful."

"I'm immune to his charm."

"You think so. And then he says something disarming, and the next thing you know you're in Vegas."

Becky laughed. "That's not going to happen."

"I'm glad you think so. What about the witness? You gonna win the fight?"

"I should. If not, I got grounds for appeal."

"Appeal?"

"Yeah. You know. The court hearing where you pay me *more* money."

"Ha, ha."

"I wasn't joking. If I can knock out the banker's testimony, I got a shot at the other witnesses."

"What other witnesses?"

"Well, there's the teller who brought him the check. But she's not a very good witness."

"How do you know?"

"If she was, they'd have put her on first. Because she's the one who saw you. The one you gave the check to. The one who can identify you as the person presenting the check. The fact she didn't means she's shaky at best."

Cora grimaced. "You're doing it again."

"What?"

"Discrediting the witnesses. The point is I never married the guy."

"Yeah, but that's hard to prove. We gotta

work with what we got."

There came a knock on the conference room door.

"We must be back in," Becky said.

She got up to go.

The door opened, and Melvin stepped in. "I hope I'm not disturbing you. Before court resumes, I thought we could have a little talk."

"I have nothing to say to you," Cora said.

"I know that. I meant with your lawyer."

Becky shook her head. "You're the opposing party. I can't talk to you directly. I should be talking to your lawyer."

Melvin smiled. "Yeah, but he won't do it. He's an old stick-in-the-mud."

"Actually, we had quite a nice talk over lunch."

"Reach an agreement? I bet he didn't even pick up the check. You wanna get anywhere, you talk right to me."

"Get anywhere? I didn't know there was anywhere to get."

"I thought you lawyers always talked settlement."

"You're offering to settle?"

"I don't know until we talk about it."

"We're not settling!" Cora said. "Becky, don't listen to him."

Fleckstein stuck his nose in the door and

spotted his client. "Oh, there you are." His eyes widened when he saw whom Melvin was with. "What are you doing? Are you crazy? You can't talk to them. For all I know, they're having the conversation recorded. Are you having the conversation recorded? If you are, I'm charging you with bad faith and bringing it before the judge. Don't talk to them. There's no reason to talk to them. It's an open-and-shut case. We're going to win, they're going to lose. That's all she wrote. What the devil are you doing talking to them?"

Melvin's eyes twinkled. He pointed at Becky. "She mentioned a settlement."

Fleckstein's mouth fell open. "She what! How dare you! How dare you, young lady! Try to settle with my client behind my back. I suppose any settlement you reach would very conveniently neglect to mention attorney fees. I'm wise to your tricks." He turned on his client. "And you, get back in the courtroom and behave. My God, it's like running a kindergarten. I should get hazard pay."

Fleckstein herded his wayward client out the door.

Becky smiled at Cora. "See? Nothing to worry about."

"Yeah," Cora snorted. "I was here and you

were saved by his attorney. Considering which, the fact you didn't wind up married to him is a rather minor achievement. Nonetheless, I'm very proud of you."

CHAPTER 28

Judge Hobbs looked as though he'd just drunk a quart of sour milk. "It appears Ms. Baldwin's objection has merit. I am very reluctantly striking the testimony of Mr. Randolph from the record. Since Mr. Randolph was responsible for identifying the check, it is also stricken from the record."

Melvin's attorney lunged to his feet.

"Sit down, Mr. Fleckstein. This is not the end of the world. Looking at your witness list, I see you have witnesses to cover the same ground. I suggest you do so. This testimony no longer exists."

Fleckstein consulted his notes. "Call Lilly Clemson."

As the witness took the stand, Cora recognized her as one of the women she'd seen in Cushman's Bake Shop. Lilly Clemson had auburn hair and wore a little too much lipstick. She stated her name and that she worked at the bank.

"Now then, Miss Clemson," Fleckstein said in a solicitous manner, "I'm going to ask you some questions about the check you showed to your employer."

"Are you going to point it out to her as well?" Becky Baldwin said. "Your Honor, this conference between attorney and witness is rather unusual. Could he confine himself to just asking questions?"

"I'm sure he meant no harm, Ms. Baldwin, but your point is well taken. Mr. Fleckstein, don't tell her what you're going to ask her, just ask."

"Yes, Your Honor. Miss Clemson, do you recall an incident when you had occasion to show a check to Mr. Randolph?"

"Yes, I do."

"Could you tell us about that?"

"Yes, I could. I received a check from Cora Felton. The Puzzle Lady. Her name's Cora Felton, but everyone knows her as the Puzzle Lady. She came in and presented a check."

"Was this unusual?"

"No. She has an account. She often brings in checks."

"Was she cashing the check?"

"No, it was for deposit."

"Did it have a deposit slip?"

"Yes, it did."

"To whose account was she depositing the check?"

"To her own. Cora Felton."

"You say she wasn't cashing the check?"

"No, just depositing it in her account."

"What did you do with the check?"

"I showed it to Mr. Randolph."

"Why?"

"Objection," Becky said. "Her thought process is not binding on the defendant."

"No, but it's relevant to her actions. If we could do without so many technical objections."

"Yes, Your Honor."

"Why did you show it to Mr. Randolph?"

"Because I was afraid there might be a problem with it."

"Now," Becky Baldwin said, "we're getting into an area where my objections might not be so technical. The witness has just suggested my client might have attempted to pass an irregular check. That is a conclusion on her part that I would object to most strongly."

"Your displeasure is noted," Judge Hobbs said. "But I'd like to hear the witness explain."

Mr. Fleckstein was smiling broadly. "And what led you to believe there might be a problem with the check?"

175

"It was deposited in Cora Felton's account, but it was not made out to Cora Felton."

"What name was it made out to?"

"Cora Felton Markowitz."

"And was it endorsed on the back?"

"Yes, it was."

"How was it endorsed?"

"Cora Felton Markowitz."

"You pointed this out to Mr. Randolph?"

"That's right."

Fleckstein held up his hand. "Now then," he said virtuously, "don't tell us what Mr. Randolph told you, but after you talked to him, what did you do with the check?"

"I deposited it to Cora Felton's account."

"Would you know that check if you saw it again?"

"Yes."

"I hand you a check marked Plaintiff's Exhibit Number One and ask if you have seen it before."

"Yes. That is the check I showed to Mr. Randolph. The one Cora Felton gave me to deposit."

"Thank you. That's all."

Judge Hobbs looked over at the defense table. "Ms. Baldwin, if you have any questions of this witness, please ask them now."

Cora Felton was tugging at Becky's sleeve.

"One moment, Your Honor," Becky said. She leaned over, whispered, "What?"

"Ask her about her relationship with Randolph."

"Why?"

"Probably be interesting."

"You're going to get me disbarred, you know it." Becky stood up and said, "Miss Clemson, what was your relationship with Mr. Randolph?"

"I beg your pardon?"

"Was he your boyfriend? Were you dating? He ever ask you out?"

"Objection, Your Honor!" Fleckstein said. "Of all the improper questions."

"It's always proper to show bias, Your Honor."

"Bias?" Fleckstein said. "How in the world does that establish bias?"

"Mr. Randolph was killed, Your Honor. If the witness was dating him, that would certainly have an effect on her testimony."

"That's not what bias means, and you know it! Your Honor, she's trying to turn the courtroom into a circus."

"I *want* to answer!"

Judge Hobbs looked at the witness in surprise. "I beg your pardon?"

"I was *not* dating Mr. Randolph. I was *never* dating Mr. Randolph. He asked me out once, but I didn't go."

"He asked you out?"

"Yes."

"How long ago was that?"

"Oh, Your Honor," Fleckstein said. "How is that relevant?"

"It probably isn't. But since the witness volunteered the information, counsel can certainly ask her about it."

"How long ago?"

"Six months ago."

"He asked you out?"

"Yes."

"And you said no?"

"Yes."

"How did he take it?"

"He seemed disappointed."

"Did his attitude towards you change in the bank?"

"No. He was very professional."

"Now, Ms. Baldwin," Judge Hobbs said, "I think we have exhausted the subject."

Becky looked at Cora as if to say, "Are you satisfied?"

Cora whispered, "Good. Now you got her rattled. Get her to admit she doesn't remember the check."

Becky looked exasperated. "I thought you were upset that I was making a fuss about the check."

"Yeah, but if you're gonna play the game, you might as well win."

Becky took a breath. "Miss Clemson, going back to the check you say you received from my client . . ."

"Well, it's about time," Fleckstein said.

Judge Hobbs banged the gavel. "If we could avoid these side comments."

"Sorry, Your Honor."

"You say my client presented you with a check."

"That's right."

"And you noticed a discrepancy in the name of the payee, so you showed it to Mr. Randolph?"

"That's right."

"And the check was presented to you by Cora Felton?"

"Yes, it was."

"I believe you said the check was made out to a Cora Felton Markowitz."

"Yes, I did."

"You pointed this out to Mr. Randolph?"

"That's right."

"Did you tell Mr. Randolph the check was made out to Cora Felton Markowitz? Or did you merely tell him it was made out to a different name?"

Lilly Clemson frowned. "I don't understand the question."

"It's a very simple question. Did you tell Mr. Randolph the name on the check was Markowitz?"

"I don't remember."

"You don't remember if you said the name Markowitz?"

"No, I don't."

"Then you probably didn't."

"Objection, Your Honor."

"Sustained."

"Did you say the name Markowitz?"

"I don't know. Is it important?"

"The truth is important. I want the truth. When you presented the check to Mr. Randolph, did you tell him the problem with it was it was made out to someone named Markowitz?"

"No."

"Objection, Your Honor!" Fleckstein jumped to his feet. "That's not what the witness means."

"That's what she said."

"Counsel is attempting to confuse the witness."

"She has every right to," Judge Hobbs said. "It may not be a shattering revelation, but it is certainly relevant. You may proceed, Ms. Baldwin."

"Thank you, Your Honor. Miss Clemson, is it not a fact that to the best of your recollection, when you showed this check to Mr. Randolph you did not use the name Markowitz?"

"Well, I guess I didn't."

"I didn't think so. You merely presented him with the check and said the names didn't exactly jibe. Is that right?"

"Yes, it is."

"You testified on direct examination that my client, Cora Felton, presented you with a check made out to Cora Felton Markowitz. Why did you say that?"

"Because she did."

"But you didn't know that."

Lilly Clemson frowned. "Huh?"

"You didn't even remember the name Markowitz, isn't that right?"

"I suppose so."

"You just testified that when my client presented the check to you, the name didn't make a big impression. You merely noticed the name was not exactly the same. And when you presented the check to Mr. Randolph, you did not even point out the name on the check was Markowitz, isn't that right?"

"Yes."

"On direct examination you testified the check was made out to Cora Felton Markowitz. Now how did you know that?"

"What do you mean?"

"If you didn't know the name Markowitz at the time, how do you know it now?"

"Well, I talked to the attorney."

"You went over your testimony with Mr. Fleckstein?"

"Objection, Your Honor. Attorneys always talk to their witnesses beforehand. There's nothing nefarious about it."

"There's nothing wrong with *talking* to witnesses. *Coaching* witnesses is something else."

"That is a slanderous accusation! Your Honor, do I have to put up with —"

The gavel silenced Fleckstein's outburst.

Judge Hobbs glared around the courtroom. "This is rapidly degenerating into a situation I do not like. Mr. Fleckstein, Ms. Baldwin's cross-examination may be vigorous, but it is certainly legal. Proceed, Ms. Baldwin."

Becky turned back to a rather flustered witness. "Miss Clemson, no one's blaming you for anything. I'm just trying to test your recollection. As I understand it, when you presented the check to Mr. Randolph, the name Markowitz didn't mean anything to you. It was only later, when you were preparing for court, that you remembered the name Markowitz. Is it fair to say that when first asked you couldn't remember the name Markowitz, and it's only after discussing the matter that you know it now? So, on direct examination, when you were asked what was the name on the check, you were able to respond, 'Cora Felton Markowitz'?"

The witness blinked several times, trying to digest all the verbiage. "I think so."

"You learned the name Markowitz so you could use it in court?"

"Objection."

"Overruled. Witness may answer."

"You learned the name Markowitz?"

"That's right."

"No further questions."

Fleckstein was on his feet. "Miss Clemson, when you say you learned the name Markowitz, you don't mean that, do you?"

The witness was taken aback. "I beg your pardon?"

"In other words, you were not *taught* the name Markowitz. It was not a new concept to you. You knew the name before. When your memory was refreshed, you *recalled* the name Markowitz, isn't that right?"

Judge Hobbs looked curiously at the defense table. "That's certainly leading and suggestive, Ms. Baldwin."

Becky smiled. "I don't want to be overly technical, Your Honor. I think we all understand the situation here."

"You knew the name Markowitz? Your recollection was merely refreshed?"

"That's right."

"That's all."

Becky rose with a smile. "Yes, Miss Clemson. And *how* was your recollection refreshed?"

"I beg your pardon?"

"Were you *told* the name Markowitz? How was the name Markowitz presented to you?"

"It was on the check."

"Made out to Cora Felton Markowitz?"

"That's right."

"The attorney showed you the check to refresh your recollection?"

"Yes."

"So," Becky said, "when you identified the check, Plaintiff's Exhibit Number One, you were identifying it not from having my client present it to you at the bank, you were identifying it from having the attorney for the plaintiff present it to you to refresh your recollection. When it was given to you in his office for you to study so you would be able to identify it on the stand."

"Objection, Your Honor!"

"Overruled. Witness may answer."

"Yes. That's where I saw the check."

"Your Honor," Becky said, "I move the

evidence, Plaintiff's Exhibit Number One, be stricken from the record. It now appears the witness cannot identify it as a check presented to her by my client, but merely as one presented to her by the plaintiff's attorney."

"Granted. The check may go out."

"Oh, Your Honor."

"Mr. Fleckstein, you will have every opportunity to resubmit it. From the evidence I just heard, the check is clearly inadmissible."

"Yes, Your Honor." Fleckstein fumbled through his papers. "Perhaps I could have a recess to adjust to this development?"

"Very well. Court is adjourned until Friday morning at ten o'clock."

Cora was pleased with the way things had gone in court until she saw Melvin looking over at the defense table with a huge grin on his face.

He wasn't looking at her.

Cora sucked in her breath.

The creep!

She glanced around just to look away and saw her nemesis, Bambi, standing in the back of the courtroom, glaring at Melvin with a look she knew well, a look she had often used on Melvin when he was still her husband, a look of frustration, exasperation,

185

irritation, and practically any other -ation she could think of — good God, why were words coming back to haunt her? She wasn't really a wordsmith. Thoughts were ping-ponging around in her head to the point of making her doubt her own sanity.

Damn it.

She hadn't felt this way since she'd been married to the louse.

CHAPTER 29

Cora, Sherry, and Aaron were having lunch in the living room and celebrating the day in court.

The only thing spoiling it was Rick Reed.

"Has there been a breakthrough in the Randolph murder case?" Rick began. "Despite the confusion surrounding the case, a person of interest has emerged. A young woman who had spurned the advances of the decedent. The facts emerged in court today, during the alimony hearing of Baker-haven's own Puzzle Lady, Cora Felton. On the witness stand, one Lilly Clemson, a teller at the bank where Mr. Randolph worked, admitted that the decedent had made advances toward her which she had spurned. It appears to be the police theory that if those advances had continued, that might be a motive. Miss Clemson declined to comment, but Police Chief Dale Harper had this to say."

The picture cut to a shot of the chief on the front steps of the police station.

"No, I don't think it had anything to do with the murder."

Rick stuck his microphone into the shot. "Then why are you investigating it?"

"We're investigating any lead, however slim. If the guy wrote a crank letter to your TV station, I'd have to check it out. It wouldn't mean we suspected you of the crime."

The camera cut back to the head shot of Rick. "Well, it's nice to know I'm in the clear, but it would also be nice to shed some light on the situation. Chief Harper claims there's none to shed. Not very promising in a homicide already over twenty-four hours old. This is Rick Reed, Channel Eight News."

Cora froze the TV, put up her hand. "Okay, this is not my fault."

Sherry looked at her. "No one said it was."

"Yeah, but if I hadn't married Melvin, and divorced Melvin, and gotten involved in an alimony dispute, and hired Becky Baldwin to represent me, and let her rip the witness apart on the stand —"

"*Let* her?" Sherry said. "It looked like you were masterminding the whole thing. What were you whispering in her ear?"

"You were in court? You should take it easy in your condition."

"I'm not in any condition!"

"That's right. You're in *no* condition. You should stay home, do some light cleaning, cook dinner."

"Should I also write your column?"

"Unless you want me to take a crack at it."

"Yeah, wouldn't that be a hoot."

"Is there anything to this business with the teller?" Aaron asked.

"Oh, no. Not you, too."

"If it's news, I need to know. That doesn't mean I'm going to write it."

"It *isn't* news," Cora said. "That's the whole point. It is *not* news. *Non-news. Un-*newsworthy."

"That's not fair," Aaron said. "You can't yell fire in a crowded theater and then blame people for running out."

"That's a horrible example."

"Why?"

"You want to hold people responsible for everything that lawyers do? It would be an utter disaster. You'd be constantly over-analyzing trivialities. It would be like what instant replay did to pro football."

"You watch pro football?"

"In my day I made a hundred bucks on a

Super Bowl."

"They had Super Bowls in your day?" Sherry said.

Cora's mouth fell open. "Oh, you're asking for it."

"You'd beat up a woman in my condition?" Sherry said.

That tripped Cora up. "Your condition? What condition?"

Sherry smiled. "See, it's no fun for you if there's nothing to push against."

"Kids," Aaron said, "it's really nice watching you spar. But we have this murder. I'd be happy for any lead."

"You and Chief Harper," Cora said.

"He's got nothing?"

"Not a damn thing."

Buddy jumped up, spun in a circle, and ran barking to the front door.

"You expecting someone?" Cora said.

"No. You hear a car in the drive?"

"No."

"Then no one should be there."

"Buddy seems to think so."

"Maybe he's wrong," Sherry said.

There came a knock on the door.

"Or maybe he's right," Cora said.

"Don't we have a doorbell?" Sherry said.

"Yes, we do," Cora said. "It can't be

anyone. If we ignore it, maybe it will go away."

"Oh, for goodness' sakes," Aaron said. "If you girls are just going to snark at each other . . ."

"Snark?" Cora said.

"You know what I mean. Sit there and keep arguing and I'll go see who it isn't."

Aaron went out and returned a moment later, ushering in the last person Cora expected to see.

Bambi.

The young woman was clearly out of her element. She had stumbled up the driveway in high heels. One shoe was slightly wobbly, which might have indicated the heel was breaking or might have merely reflected the fact that she'd had too much to drink. She swayed unsteadily and fought to keep her balance, while the toy poodle darted in and out around her feet as if she were his best friend ever.

"He's precious. Can I take him home?"

"Not going to happen," Cora told her.

Bambi blew the hair out of her eyes in a gesture men undoubtedly found cute and declared, "You don't like me."

"Now, there's a remarkable insight."

"Of course you don't," Bambi said complacently. "I'm with Melvin now. I under-

191

stand. You still like him. But you can't have him. So you don't like me."

"Well, you're half-right," Cora said.

Bambi crinkled her nose. "Huh?"

"Why are you here?"

Bambi pulled a piece of paper out of her purse. "I have a puzzle."

Cora could not have been more surprised had Bambi whipped out a pistol and begun spraying the room. "*You* have a puzzle?"

"Hey, just because I'm pretty doesn't mean I'm not smart. I can do sudoku."

"I'll alert the media," Cora said.

"Are you mocking me? You don't like me because I'm young and pretty, but that's no reason to mock me."

"No, I'm sure there are others," Cora said. "What's this about a puzzle?"

"It's a number puzzle. But it's not a sudoku."

Bambi gave the puzzle to Cora.

3÷		30x	1−	10+	
1−				1−	
3−		12x		5−	
5+		4−		15x	
3−	1−		4−		2÷
	5−		1−		

"Oh, it's a KenKen. That's why you can't do it."

"I can do a KenKen. You think I can't add and subtract?"

"I'm sure you can multiply. So why are you here?"

"I didn't want to wake Melvin up. Melvin's sleeping."

"Ah," Cora said. "Sleeping. At this time of day that's a euphemism for passed out."

"Anyway, I could do it just fine if I hadn't

been having a drink." Bambi cocked her head, tried to keep it from tipping too far to one side. "*I've* been having a drink."

"Hadn't noticed," Cora said.

"So I brought it to you."

"Hold on. You probably don't realize it, but you're not making any sense. Why are you bringing me a puzzle at all?"

"Because I want to know what it means."

"It doesn't mean anything. It's a KenKen. It's a bunch of numbers."

"And I want to know what the numbers mean."

"Why in the world would the numbers mean anything?"

"I don't know."

"Oh, for goodness' sakes," Sherry said impatiently. "You mind if I jump in here? I *haven't* been married to Melvin, so I can still think straight. Bambi, where did you get the KenKen? Why do you think it's important?"

"Great," Cora said. "You ask her *two* questions. We'll be here all night while she sorts that out. Bambi, where did you get the Ken-Ken?"

"Under the door."

"Someone slipped it under the door of your room at the motel?"

"That's right."

"Just like this? Or was it in something?"

"It was in an envelope."

"Was the envelope addressed to you?"

"No."

"Who was it addressed to?"

"Nobody."

"It didn't say anything on the envelope?"

"No."

"Then what makes you think it means something?"

"Because it had this with it."

Bambi reached in her purse and pulled out a crossword puzzle.

ACROSS

1   Never let go of
5   Masked man
10 Oodles
14 History chapters
15 Disney's middle name
16 Neck of the woods

17 Online convenience
18 Message, part 1
20 Brain size?
21 Turns tail
22 Ohio city
23 In-tray item
25 Intruded, with "in"
26 Message, part 2
31 Sounds from Santa
32 Wooden shoe
33 Water _____
37 "The Plague" setting
38 Casting need
39 Not fooled by
40 Aardvark snacks
41 CIA agent, in slang
43 RBIs, for instance
44 Message, part 3
46 Keanu Reeves thriller, with "The"
50 Like a Visa balance
51 Language characteristic
52 Out of sorts?
55 Novelist Tan
58 Message, part 4
60 Ophthalmologist's concern
61 Ship that sailed in quest of the Golden Fleece
62 Holmes or Couric
63 Rope fiber
64 Pro in futures?

65 Edit
66 Häagen-Dazs alternative

DOWN

1 Brown seaweed
2 A Great Lake
3 Jipijapa topper
4 "For shame!"
5 Extremists
6 Like ye shoppe
7 Sally into space?
8 Charlie Brown cry
9 _____ Kosh B'Gosh
10 Las Vegas gambler
11 Long-armed ape
12 Prove false
13 Dieter's lunch
19 Midterm, e.g.
21 Some radios
24 Collar types
25 On the other hand
26 Stop order
27 Traffic blast
28 Zeppo and Gummo's brother
29 Online publication
30 Part of "Funiculi, Funicula" song refrain
33 Lawgiver, in Hebrew
34 Preceded in time

35 _____-Tass (Russian news agency)
36 Memo
41 Boston Red _____
42 Having round protuberances
44 Arm or leg
45 _____-night doubleheader
46 King with a golden touch
47 Be gaga over
48 Bit of color
49 Chopper's chopper
52 Man on first?
53 Guitar relative
54 Words with an ante
56 "Well, I declare!"
57 Cowboy affirmatives
59 Barely manage, with "out"
60 My fair lady?

CHAPTER 30

Bambi was tipsy enough that, it wasn't hard to perform the sleight of hand that made it look as though Cora and not Sherry had solved the crossword. While Cora kept Bambi occupied with the KenKen, Sherry knocked off the puzzle in the next room. Cora hardly had to vamp at all, though at one point she was so slow at making a calculation, Bambi tried to grab the pencil.

When Sherry came back, Cora whipped into the office, picked up the crossword puzzle, and read it over.

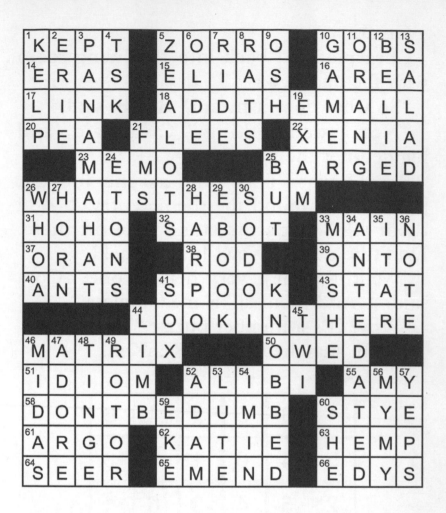

The theme entry was, "Add them all. What's the sum? Look in there. Don't be dumb."

Wonderful.

What was she supposed to make of that?

Was there anything else in the puzzle that might give a hint?

No, there wasn't.

No reference to any particular line of the KenKen or any relevance it might have.

Great.

Cora plodded back into the living room with the bad news.

"So what does it mean?" Bambi said.

"Not a damn thing," Cora said, and handed her the puzzle.

Bambi wasn't as slow as she looked, because she found the theme entry. " 'Add them all. What's the sum? Look in there. Don't be dumb.' Wow! It is a clue!"

"Well, it's not a very helpful one," Cora said. " 'Add them all' is meaningless."

"Why? It's a number puzzle."

Bambi snatched up the KenKen.

1	3	5	2	4	6
5	4	6	1	2	3
2	5	4	3	6	1
4	1	2	6	3	5
6	2	3	5	1	4
3	6	1	4	5	2

"Yeah. It's a 6-by-6 KenKen," Cora said. "Every line will have the numbers 1 through

6. That's what, ten, fifteen, twenty-one per row. Times six is a hundred twenty-six. Every single KenKen will be exactly the same."

"That's pretty stupid," Bambi said.

Cora looked at Sherry. "Notice my restraint."

"It only adds up to that because you solved it," Bambi said. "It wouldn't add up to that if you *didn't* solve it."

"No. It would add up to zero. Because a KenKen's not like a sudoku. A sudoku starts with some of the numbers filled in. A KenKen doesn't start with any numbers."

"Yes, it does."

"No, it doesn't."

"It does so. It's full of little numbers."

"What? Oh, those aren't the numbers in the squares. Those are the numbers telling what the numbers in the squares should add up to."

"So?"

"So what?"

"Add 'em up."

"Why?"

"You got a better idea?"

"I've got no idea at all. Of course, nobody gave me this puzzle."

"I did."

"You *brought* it to me. No one *sent* it to

me. It was not *intended* for me. It was intended for you and he whose name one dare not speak."

"You talk funny."

"Right back at you, kid. The point is if this has any meaning for you, you can't expect me to know what it is."

"Except you were married to Melvin," Sherry said cheerfully. "You have a single point of reference."

"Thank you," Cora said dryly. "That's a big help. Anyway, if I add this up, I get . . . ninety-three. What does the number ninety-three mean?"

"The year she was born?" Sherry suggested.

"You're not helping," Cora said.

"The difference in your ages?"

"I'll throw you out of here."

Sherry shook her head. "We're not leaving the two of you alone together. If Bambi were found torn limb from limb, you wouldn't be able to prove you didn't do it."

"Whereas if *you* were found torn limb from limb —"

"Come on," Aaron said. "Solve this thing."

"There's nothing to solve."

"I don't buy that. You're just saying that because it's her. If anyone else had brought you the puzzle, you'd have solved it by now."

"Why, Aaron Grant. Sherry, looks like your hubby just grew a pair."

"He's just showing off for Bambi," Sherry said.

Aaron threw up his hands. "I've done it. Now they're ganging up on me. How about it, girls? Let's make some sense out of all this. I *need* the story."

"Oh, well, when you put it that way," Cora said. "I wasn't trying before, but if you *need* a story . . . Okay. Say the number's gotta mean something. What's ninety-three?"

Bambi, who had been laboriously adding up the numbers in the puzzle, said, "It's not ninety-three. It's a hundred and six."

"Oh, for God's sake! It's ninety-three. I added it up."

"You added it wrong."

Cora couldn't believe the girl was arguing with her. "Oh, look here —"

"It *is* a hundred and six," Sherry said.

"What!" Cora said.

"Believe it or not. I just did it myself."

Cora glowered at her niece. "Fine. So it's a hundred and six. Big deal. What's a hundred and six?"

"One more than a hundred and five," Bambi said.

"Gee, thanks," Cora said. "That clears it up."

"Well, it's true," Bambi said.

"Yeah, it's true. A hundred and six is one more than a hundred and five. And what's a hundred and five?"

"Our motel room."

CHAPTER 31

"Are you comfortable leaving Aaron with Bambi?" Cora asked as she and Sherry drove out to the Oakwood Motel.

"I wasn't going to let you go alone."

"That's thoughtful of you."

"It wasn't thoughtful of me. I don't trust you not to get in trouble."

"That isn't thoughtful?"

"How do you plan to get into the room?"

"I thought we'd drive up to the door and knock."

"Bambi says no one's there."

"You really want to quote Bambi as an authority on anything? So she says no one's there. Let's see if she's right."

"What if someone opens the door?"

"Then we get in."

"What if Bambi's right and the place isn't rented?"

"Then we rent it."

"What?"

"You got a credit card, don't you? Just rent the damn thing."

"We can't rent a motel room."

"Why not?"

"We have a house."

"So what? You're a newlywed. You had a fight with your husband."

"I did not!"

"You think they're gonna check?"

"I don't want people going around thinking Aaron and I are fighting."

"No one's going around. We're just renting a room."

"It better be for another reason."

"Fine. It's for another reason."

"What's the reason?"

"What?"

"You got a reason for renting the room?"

"Yes."

"What is it?"

"Because I *want* one! Good God, you're the most squeamish accomplice. Becky Baldwin wasn't this bad."

"What?"

"When you were on your honeymoon, Becky did some snooping. I thought *she* was a pain."

"She's a lawyer. She wouldn't let you *do* outrageous things."

"You'd be surprised. Ah, here we are."

Cora drove right by the front desk and pulled into the parking lot. There was no car in front of 106.

"Looks like no one's there," Sherry said.

"We'll verify that."

Cora pulled up right into the space, stopped the car, and got out. She walked up to 106, banged on the door.

"Do we rent it?" Sherry said.

"Guess so."

Cora twisted the doorknob.

It clicked open.

Sherry grabbed Cora's arm. "Don't go in there!"

"What?"

"I don't like it. This is where they always find the dead body."

"Who does?"

"People in movies."

"This isn't a movie."

"You know what I mean. You don't wanna open that door."

"The problem is, I do."

Cora pushed open the door, stepped inside.

Sherry hesitated a moment.

Cora grabbed her arm, yanked her in, and slammed the door.

"Hey!"

"Shut up! Keep your voice down! Melvin's

in the next room!"

"Yeah, but —"

"Look!"

Sherry looked where Cora was pointing.

On the floor, in plain sight, was a revolver.

Sherry sucked in her breath. "Is that the murder weapon?"

"Bet you a nickel. It looks like a .45-caliber. From the smell, it's been fired."

Sherry reached in her purse, whipped out her cell phone.

"What are you doing?"

"Calling the police."

Cora snatched the phone. "Oh, no, you're not."

"We have to."

"Why?"

"Why? We just found evidence."

"How do you know it's evidence?"

"Don't get cute with me. It's evidence, and you know it."

"Yeah, but you don't like that. Trust me, you'll be much happier if you take the position that it *isn't* evidence."

"Cora, this is not a game. This is a murder case, and we have to cooperate with the police."

"And we *will*. But we have to be careful how we do it."

"Why?"

"You haven't thought this through. If we call the cops, what's gonna happen?"

"They're gonna come here, they're gonna take the evidence, end of story."

"No, it's not the end of the story. Then they're gonna grill Bambi and arrest Melvin. On the grounds they had the murder weapon."

"But they didn't."

"Yes, they did. Look at it from the police's point of view. Bambi comes and gets us, feeds us a load of crap, practically forces us to search the motel unit. Why? Because she realized Melvin had it, got cold feet, and wanted a way out."

"That's really stupid."

"Well, Bambi isn't very smart."

"Come on, Cora, you can't have it both ways. She can't be clever enough to plan this, and too stupid to plan it well. That's the type of thing you always say, only it's Melvin, so you can't think straight."

"I'm thinking straight, damn it. I'm thinking just fine. If you call Chief Harper, you know what he's gonna do? He's gonna arrest Melvin. With all the pressure on him to come up with something, he can't help it. It doesn't matter if he can make it stick. The fact is, he'll have to haul him in with the media attention and the whole bit. What will happen then?"

"You'll throw a party and laugh yourself sick."

Cora shook her head pityingly. "You're the one who isn't thinking. He'll find himself accused of murder. He'll hire an attorney."

"He *has* an attorney."

"He has a *divorce* lawyer. You think little Mr. Shysterpants ever handled a murder case? He'll need a criminal attorney. He'll hire Becky Baldwin."

"He can't do that."

"Why not?"

"She'll turn him down."

"Yeah, right. Becky's really in a position to turn down a six-figure retainer."

"Six-figure?"

"Melvin's got it. Melvin's always got money. Anyway, he'll tie up Becky Baldwin so she can't represent me in the alimony suit."

"But you hired her first."

"Right. I'm sure that will be a point in my favor when I stand up to Melvin and say, 'No, you can't have her, I had her first,' while Becky is saying, 'Yes, he can.' "

"You're not going to turn over the gun?"

"Of course I'm going to turn over the gun. I'm just not going to turn it over like this."

"So, what are you going to do?"

"The same thing you're going to do. I'm going to go back to the house, look Bambi straight in the eye, and tell her we searched the motel room and couldn't find a thing."

CHAPTER 32

Bambi was incredulous. "Nothing?"

"Absolutely nothing. A hundred and six must mean something else."

Bambi scrunched up her nose. "I don't understand."

"There's nothing to understand. There was nothing there."

Aaron had been feeding Bambi coffee and she seemed to have sobered up. "That's stupid. With so much coincidence, it must be true."

"What coincidence?" Cora said.

"Well, the letter. Coming under our door. In one oh five. And telling us to look in one oh six."

"It doesn't really tell us to look in one oh six."

"It adds up to one oh six."

"That was your idea. It's just a theory. There are other theories."

"Like what?"

"One oh six could be a post office box number."

"That's silly."

"The idea the numbers add up at all is far-fetched."

"But the crossword said —"

"Yes, it did. Let me take another look at the puzzle."

Cora scanned the crossword, looking for something she could point to.

The word *main* jumped out at her.

"Look at that," Cora said.

"What?"

"33 Across. Main. We have a Main Street in town."

"Every town has a Main Street."

"Every town doesn't have a murder and a crossword puzzle and a KenKen."

Cora slapped the puzzle on the coffee table, headed for the door.

"Where are you going?" Bambi said.

"To check out this lead."

"What lead? There's no lead. What are you talking about, 'this lead'?"

"Sherry, come with me. Aaron, keep feeding her coffee. You're doing a great job."

Sherry ran after Cora, hopped into the car as Cora took off down the drive. "Where are you going?"

"I'm following this new lead. One oh six

Main Street. It seems very promising. I want to check it out."

"Slow down. What's the hurry?"

"I want to get there before Bambi over-powers your hubby and catches up with us."

"That's not going to happen."

"You don't know for sure. Women have an amazing amount of strength where Melvin is involved. They can bench-press five times their own body weight."

"Cora."

"What's the street number of the police station?"

"I never noticed."

"Me either. It would be embarrassing if it was one oh six. But I don't think it has a number. I think it just says 'Police Station.' I mean, it's not that it doesn't *have* a number, I'm sure it *has* a number, it's just that it doesn't *say* the number."

"Watch the road, will you?"

"I'm driving just fine. But you're right. It would be a hell of a time to get pulled over."

Cora cruised into town. The police station was indeed without a number. But the library across the street was 11.

"There you are," Cora said. "The police station must be ten or twelve or something. And, yes, the drugstore's eighteen. The numbers go up as you go out of town."

Cora drove along Main. A half mile out of town, the houses got farther apart.

"Here we go. Let's see, ninety-six, a hundred, a hundred and two, a hundred and eight."

Cora slammed on the brakes. The car skidded to a stop.

"No hundred and six?" Sherry said.

"Shut up."

"Gee, it was such a good theory."

"It's still a good theory."

"How?"

"It's a two-way street."

"What?"

Cora wrenched the wheel through a U-turn, sped back toward town. Slowed as she neared the library.

"Okay, here we go. Eleven. Seven. Five. And we're at the corner. Look. See? The numbers start up again."

"This is North Street," Sherry said.

"North *Main* Street."

"It's North Street."

"So what? It's the same street. Did we turn a corner? No. We're going in a straight line."

"I don't recall the word *north* in the puzzle."

"I don't either."

"So what made you try this way?"

"Because it wasn't that way."

"Cora."

"Sherry, I've got a gun in my purse. Actually, two guns. One I always have. The other is superfluous. I've gotta get rid of it. I'd like to do that without making us accessories to a murder. Which we would be if I threw it in the woods. Which is starting to look more and more tempting."

"Don't you dare."

"Well, then, stop with the North Street. I *know* it's North Street. I'm doing the best I can."

They had reached a stretch of meadowland where the mailboxes were infrequent and the houses were set back from the road.

"Seventy-five. Good. All right, here we go. What's that number? Ninety-four. Come on, one oh six. Come on, one oh six."

"You sound like you're in Vegas."

"I wish I were in Vegas."

"What's the next number? Ninety-eight. Every four numbers. Good. One oh two, one oh six. Come on. Come on. And the next mailbox is . . ."

A hundred.

"Damn! That throws the whole thing off!"

The next mailbox was 102.

"Back on track!"

Cora flashed around a curve. There was a

driveway at the top of a hill.

"If that's one oh eight, I'm going to lose it."

It was 106.

Cora hit the brakes, screeched into a turn, stopped at the mailbox. In front of her was a two-story frame house with no car in the drive.

"Good. Perfect."

Cora jumped out of the car, raced to the mailbox, and jerked it open.

It was full of mail.

Well, nothing she could do about that now.

Cora reached in her purse, pulled out a gun, thrust it into the mailbox. Pulled it out, double-checked to make sure it was the right one. It was. She put it back in the mailbox and snapped it shut. She took a breath, opened the mailbox, pulled out the gun. She ran back to the car and hopped in.

"Sherry. We have to go to the police. I just found a gun."

CHAPTER 33

Chief Harper could not have looked more skeptical had Cora attempted to sell him snake oil.

"You found this gun in a mailbox?"

"That's right."

"On North Street?"

"North Main Street."

"It's just called North Street."

"Oh."

"And how did you come to find it?"

"I'm not prepared to answer that."

"What!"

"There's a gray area here, Chief. I don't want to get into any trouble."

"You don't want to get into any trouble? You're bringing me a gun which is most likely the murder weapon and you won't tell me how you found it and you don't want to get into any trouble?"

"I'm glad you understand the situation."

A vein was bulging in Chief Harper's

forehead. "I *don't* understand the situation. I was trying to *ridicule* the idea that I understood the situation."

"That's a little harsh on you, Chief. You're usually very good at understanding."

"Cora, so help me, I will come over the desk and strangle you."

"A very inadvisable move, Chief. I can't see any way that would play well on TV."

"Just what do you think you're doing?"

"I'm trying to fulfill my civic duty by placing in your hands the evidence that your investigation should have. I mean to cooperate with you in every way."

Chief Harper picked up the plastic Ziploc bag in which Cora had delivered the gun. "If this turns out to be the murder weapon, and there is every indication it will, then you had in your possession the very gun used to kill a key witness against you in your trial."

"It's not a trial, Chief. Just an alimony hearing."

"I don't care if it's a clambake. The witness was shot dead. There's the gun. You had it. You won't explain. You expect me to be happy?"

Cora put up her hand. "To be fair, Chief, I do not expect you to be happy. Even though I've done you a big favor by bring-

221

ing you the gun."

"Just what do you expect me to do with it?"

"Well, I'm not the chief of police, but if I were you, I would run it down to the lab in Danbury and see if it matches up with the fatal bullet."

"Yeah, great." Harper mopped his brow. "The public and the media are screaming for blood. The prosecutor's needling me to make an arrest. And all I've got is you."

"Whoa. Nasty situation. I suppose I should call my lawyer."

"You don't need a lawyer."

"What is that, Chief, a reverse Miranda warning? 'You have the right to keep talking and not hire an attorney?' Ratface is going to love you for that."

"That's not what I mean and you know it."

"Even so, I think I wanna speak to my lawyer. I do get one phone call, don't I?"

Chief Harper sat seething while Cora dialed the phone.

"Becky, Cora. I'm in the police station surrendering what looks like the murder weapon, and the police aren't happy with my answers to their questions. Wanna swing by? . . . Okay, thanks." Cora hung up the phone. "She told me to shut up, she'll be right over."

"Great."

Becky's office was just around the corner. She made it in two minutes flat.

"You stop to put on your lipstick?" Cora said.

"I'd like to talk to my client alone and in private."

"That won't be necessary," Harper said.

"Apparently it will. If I understand the situation, my client has brought you a key piece of evidence, in return for which she has been subjected to a grueling cross-examination. Under the circumstances, I'm advising my client to make no statement until I've had a chance to confer with her."

"The grueling cross-examination consisted of me asking her where she got the gun."

"Potato, potato," Becky said. "Come on, Cora, let's have a little chat."

Harper gave the women a disgusted look, went out, and closed the door.

Once they were alone, Becky said, "What gives?"

Cora gave Becky a rundown of the situation.

"The evidence points to *Melvin?*" Becky said.

"He got what appears to be a blackmail note."

"How is that a blackmail note?"

"It points to the gun."

"The gun was next door."

"Exactly. Because the blackmail note doesn't say where he has the gun. It says where he ditched it."

Becky frowned. "That's pretty far-fetched."

"No fair. Anytime you mix a crossword puzzle and a KenKen in with a murder, it's bound to be far-fetched."

"It still has to make sense on its own level."

"I know," Cora said. "And this doesn't. It doesn't make any sense at all. And you know what that means. The police will ignore all subtleties and go straight for the obvious. They'll wind up arresting Melvin."

"So?"

"And you can't represent him."

"Why not?"

"Because you're representing me."

"Oh, for goodness' sakes."

"What?"

"So that's your plan. To hold out on the police so they'll hassle you, so I'll have to represent you, so I'll be tied up and I can't represent him."

"You have a keen legal mind."

"What makes you think I'd represent him in the first place?"

"You're an attorney. A professional bottom-dweller. You'll represent anybody."

"That isn't true."

"You represented Dennis."

"That's different."

"How is that different?"

"I wasn't representing Sherry."

"Then it's a good thing you're representing me."

"I was *already* representing you."

"Not for the murder."

"Are you really afraid Melvin is going to get charged with murder and try to hire me?"

"Yeah."

"What if he did? What's the worst that can happen?"

"The worst that can happen is he marries you and ruins your life."

"He's already married."

"That's never stopped him before."

"Okay. Say I represent him for murder. What's the *second* worst thing that can happen?"

"You get him off."

CHAPTER 34

"So," Becky said, "my client would like to make a statement."

"I can't wait."

"My client is making a statement voluntarily and of her own free will. Purely because she wishes to aid the police in their investigation."

"She's a saint," Harper said. "Get on with it."

"She is making it with the understanding that there will be no attempt to prosecute her or hold her liable in any way for failing to make a statement earlier. She merely wished, as is her right, to have a chance to confer with her attorney."

"Even though she's done nothing wrong," Chief Harper said ironically.

"That goes without saying. But since you've said it, let's reiterate it. My client is blameless for any initial reluctance to share the rather bizarre circumstances surrounding the finding of this gun."

"Granted. What are the circumstances?"

Cora produced the crossword puzzle and the KenKen.

Harper looked them over. "So?"

"That's what led me to the gun."

"How in the name of heaven does that lead you to the gun?"

"My client will explain if you'll let her. I can't promise you're going to like the explanation."

"I'm sure I won't like the explanation. What is it?"

Cora explained how the crossword puzzle suggested the numbers in the KenKen be added. "Since the numbers in the solution would always add up to the same thing, we tried adding the numbers in the problem."

"The what?" Harper said.

Cora explained adding the numbers and getting 106. "Since that wasn't particularly helpful, I looked around to see if there was any other hint in the puzzle. I found the word *main.* So I figured the answer was one oh six Main Street."

"The mailbox was one oh six *North* Street."

"One oh six North *Main* Street."

"It's just North Street. How in the world did you wind up at one oh six North

227

Street?"

"Because there wasn't any one oh six Main Street. So I turned around and went out of town in the other direction until I hit one oh six. You say that's one oh six North. To me it's one oh six Main. Anyway, here's the gun."

Harper frowned. "I don't like it."

"I hate it like hell. But it's my civic duty, so here it is."

"All right. Where'd you get the puzzles?"

Cora grimaced. "Now we get into hearsay evidence, which I know you don't want."

"Now we get into locking up the witness until she cooperates, which I know you don't want."

"Was that a threat?" Becky said. "I certainly hope that wasn't a threat."

"Oh, come on. My nerves are frayed. Drop the legal mumbo jumbo and tell me what happened. Where'd you get the puzzles?"

"They were given to me," Cora said. "That's why it's hearsay."

"It's not hearsay who *gave* them to you. Who was it?"

"Melvin's wife."

"You're kidding!"

"See," Cora said. "You tell the truth, and all you get is skepticism and disbelief.

228

Melvin's wife came to me very upset. Someone had put these puzzles in an envelope and slipped them under the motel room door."

"She brought them to you?"

"Yes."

"What did your ex-husband have to say about that?"

"He didn't know."

"Why not?"

"Now," Cora said, "this is where you're getting into hearsay and speculation. I only know what she told me, and I can't vouch for any of it. But according to Melvin's wife, he was in bed passed out. She didn't know what to do, she panicked, and brought it to me."

"Without telling Melvin?"

"She knew he wouldn't let her. He's my ex-husband. He's suing me in court. He wouldn't let her come near me."

"But she did anyway."

"She wanted to know what the puzzles meant. After all, someone is dead."

"And through the most convoluted logic possible, this led you to a gun. Why in the world is Melvin connected to the gun?"

"I don't believe he is."

"You don't?"

"Of course not. It's absolutely absurd. The

man kills his own witness?"

"Yes, but we don't know why."

"What do you mean, why? There isn't any why. The guy's on Melvin's side. He testified for him on the stand."

"Suppose he was going to recant his testimony?" Harper suggested.

"About approving a check? What would that do? It would be a minor hiccup at best. All Melvin would have to do is what he's doing now. Call other people to the stand."

"Which may not work. The way I understand it, Becky made mincemeat of the other witness."

"Even so, it's a ridiculous idea."

Harper thought that over. "Okay. I guess I gotta talk to Melvin's wife. Where is she?"

"At our house."

"Oh?"

"Aaron's with her."

"Alone?"

"Sherry must be back by now. She dropped me off here."

Harper picked up the phone and dialed. "Sherry? . . . Chief Harper. Is Melvin's wife there? . . . Okay, thanks." Harper hung up. "She went back to the motel."

He raised his head and bellowed, "Dan!"

"You have an intercom, don't you, Chief?" Cora said.

Harper glared at her.

Dan Finley stuck his head in the door. "Yeah, Chief?"

"Go out to the — What's the name of the motel?"

"Oakwood."

"Go out to the Oakwood Motel, pick up Mrs. Crabtree, and bring her in. I got some questions to ask her."

"Can I help you question her?" Cora said brightly.

"I don't think so," Harper said. "Why don't you run along."

"Killjoy. Come on, Becky. Let's go."

"Reverse psychology?" Becky said on the way back to her office.

"I didn't really want to be there when the bimbo comes in."

"Petty jealousy?"

"Not entirely."

"You know, you could have helped Dan Finley out by giving him the room number."

"I didn't want to."

"Why not?"

"I don't want to give anyone ideas."

"What do you mean?"

"It's too close to some other numbers I could think of."

"Damned if it isn't."

CHAPTER 35

Becky shook her head. "I don't like this."

"It's not so bad."

"The hell it isn't. Sherry's a witness. Not to mention a co-conspirator."

"Hey, it's better than Bambi."

"Cora, I'm not Sherry's lawyer. I can't *be* Sherry's lawyer."

"Why not?"

"I'm her ex-husband's lawyer."

"Good. Remember that when Melvin tries to hire you."

"Cora, this is no laughing matter."

"That's why I'm not laughing."

"You moved the gun."

"Of course I moved the gun. I brought it to the police station."

"You moved the place you found it."

"I would have to dispute that. I don't think anyone could accuse me of moving the motel room. This is not the end of the world. If little Miss Ditsy Pants tells the cops the KenKen added up to a number that was *almost* her room number, I don't think anybody's going to be surprised that it didn't pan out."

"Whereas no one will have a problem with North Main Street," Becky said sarcastically.

"North Main Street is far more credible than room one oh six."

"How do you figure that?"

"Because a gun was found there. That immediately ratchets up the credibility. Whereas *nothing* was found in the motel room. It's hardly credible at all."

"The gun *was* found in the motel room."

"No one knows that. And no one has to know that. Because if they did, they'd be arresting Melvin for murder, and that's never a good thing. If you accuse a man of murder, he's got nothing to lose, and he lashes out in all directions, and I'm one of them. So if we could just downplay the gun in the motel room . . ."

"Downplay?" Becky said. "What a charming suggestion of how to handle tampering with evidence, compounding a felony, and conspiring to conceal a crime. Let's *downplay* it."

"Well, I wouldn't play it up," Cora said. "Of course, you're the attorney."

The phone rang.

Becky glared at Cora, snatched it up. "Hello? . . . Sorry, Chief, didn't mean to snap. I'm a little on edge. . . . What's that? . . . No, that can't be right. . . . No, I'm not arguing with you, Chief. We'll be right there."

Becky slammed down the phone, put her hands on her hips. "Well, now we're screwed."

"What's the matter?"

"Dan Finley brought in Melvin's wife."

"And?"

"She just made a statement. Guess what she said?"

"That the puzzles referred to the motel and I must have found the gun in room one oh six?"

Becky smiled grimly. "No. She says she never gave you any puzzles at all."

CHAPTER 36

Cora nipped at Becky's heels as she strode down the alley to the police station. "I've got witnesses, Becky. Granted, they're biased, but that goes to the weight, not the admissibility, right? If they had to testify? They were there. They saw her give me the puzzles. They heard what she said. I swear to you, I'm not making it up."

"Like one oh six North Street."

"Okay, maybe I made that up. But the rest of it's sound. I mean, why would I drag the bimbo into it if I didn't have to?"

"She's young and pretty and you hate her guts?"

"That has nothing to do with it."

"Of course not. It's true. Truth has very little to do with any of it."

Becky marched up the steps, threw open the front door of the police station, strode inside.

Dan Finley stuck his head out the door of

Chief Harper's office and waved to them. "Come on in." Under his breath, he added, "He's not happy."

Cora followed Becky into the office and stopped dead.

Standing next to the desk was an attractive woman of approximately thirty years of age, with flaming red hair and flashing green eyes. "Is that her?" she demanded. "Is that the woman spreading all the lies?"

"Who are you?" Cora said.

"I'm Melvin's wife. His current wife. His legal wife. As opposed to his ex-wife, the one who's bleeding him dry."

"You're Melvin's wife?"

"Are you hard of hearing? You're not that old. Well, maybe you are. Damn right I'm his wife. How *dare* you tell lies about me to the police?"

"I never said a word about you."

"Oh, yeah? You sent an officer to pick me up."

"Are you staying at the Oakwood Motel?"

"I certainly am."

"You're not staying with Melvin."

"That's none of your damn business. I'll thank you to butt out of my personal affairs. Which includes giving misinformation to the police."

Cora collapsed into a chair. "Oh, for

God's sake."

"You want to clue me in?" Chief Harper said.

"My ex-husband is every bit the son of a bitch he always was. This may be his legally married wife, but he's not traveling with her. He's got a younger, fresher bimbo in tow."

"Is that true?" Harper demanded of Mrs. Crabtree.

"I fail to see how my marital problems are any concern of the police."

"This is a murder investigation. We wanted to question the woman staying with Melvin at the Oakwood Motel. We assumed that was you. If it's not, we apologize, but it's hardly our fault."

"You might ask her what she's doing staying at the same motel as her husband and his current flame."

"Oh, I'm sure I'll have some questions." Harper bellowed, "Dan!"

"I'm right here, Chief."

"Oh. Then I don't have to explain the situation. Would you like to try again? Go to the Oakwood Motel and bring me the woman residing in the room with Melvin Crabtree."

"Would you like Melvin, too?"

"Not if you can possibly avoid it. I see

nothing to be gained by a family reunion."

"Well, you're not going to get it," Mrs. Crabtree said. "If you had no reason to bring me in, then you have no reason to hold me. I'm out of here."

"You're not going to ask her any questions?" Cora said.

"Yes, I am. Mrs. Crabtree, were you aware that your husband was staying at the same motel you were?"

"Of course."

"Were you aware that a young lady was staying with him?"

"Yes, I was aware of it."

"And was he aware you were staying at the same motel?"

"What do you think?"

"I know what I think. I'm asking you."

"No, he was not."

"And I assume the young lady in question wasn't either."

"One would assume."

"I have a question," Cora said. "Did you take care to *see* that they were not aware of your presence?"

"Yes, I did."

"In other words, you were spying on them. Were you aware your husband was here for an alimony suit?"

"Yes, of course."

"Do you have any opinion as to that?"

"Yes. I hope he wins it."

"Why?"

"The less money he pays you, the more he'll have to pay me."

"You're planning on filing for divorce?"

"You think I want to remain in this deplorable situation?"

"So, you're here primarily to dig up evidence to use in a divorce case."

"That's one way to look at it."

"What's another?"

Mrs. Crabtree frowned. "I think I've answered all the questions I need to."

"I think so," Harper said.

"I'm not so sure," Cora said.

"What do you mean?"

"Well, if she didn't receive the items in question, you have to wonder if she was the one who sent them."

"Interesting," Harper said.

"What items in question?" Melvin's wife said. "What are you talking about?"

"If you actually did send them," Cora said, "pretending not to know what they were would be a good course of action."

"I don't think I need to answer any more of your questions. I *know* I don't have to answer yours." The fiery redhead straightened, stuck out her chin, and strode off.

"You going to let her walk out?" Cora said.

"How do you suggest I stop her?"

"Hold her on suspicion of something."

"Suspicion of what?"

"Suspicion of using henna rinse. What the hell does it matter?"

"It matters when some low-life lawyer sues me. No offense meant."

"None taken," Becky said.

"You wouldn't represent her, would you?" Cora said.

"I don't know. Does she have money?"

"You're not helping. The woman's getting away."

"Do you want her here when the other woman shows up?" Harper said.

"It might be interesting."

"It might be chaotic. It's bad enough having you here. I don't need *three* women fighting over the same man."

"I'm not *fighting* over Melvin! I have no *interest* in Melvin! The women are *welcome to* Melvin!"

"It's a small office. I can hear you just fine."

"Would you like us to leave?" Becky suggested.

"Stick around. Who knows what Dan will bring back this time."

The second time Dan got it right. Fifteen

minutes later, he ushered in Bambi.

The young woman sized up the present company and twisted her lips into a pout.

"Do you know why you're here?" Harper said.

"Yeah." Bambi jerked her thumb at Cora. "She ratted me out."

"I mean did Dan explain why we want to talk to you?"

"No. He just said you did. I'd have argued with him, but I didn't want to wake Melvin."

"Considerate of you," Harper said. "I understand you got a letter."

"I didn't get a letter. I got a crossword puzzle and a number puzzle."

"A KenKen," Cora said.

"Whatever. It was slipped under the door. I didn't know what to do with it, so I brought it to her. She said it didn't mean anything. If it didn't mean anything, why am I here?"

"The puzzle led Ms. Felton to an address at the edge of town. There was a mailbox at the end of the driveway. There was a gun in the mailbox."

Bambi's mouth fell open. "There was what!"

"There was a gun in the mailbox. We won't know until the forensic tests are done, but it might be the gun that killed Mr. Randolph."

"That can't be true."

"Why not?"

"It makes no sense."

"It makes no sense because we don't know the facts. Once the facts are known . . ."

"What facts? What mailbox? Whose house was this?"

"The house belongs to a Mr. and Mrs. Prichert. They've been residents of Baker-haven for over forty years. They have three grown children, all of whom have left home. She's a retired school-teacher. He's a retired farm equipment salesman. The chance that either of them is involved in the murder of a banker seems rather slim."

Bambi crinkled her nose. "Then what was a gun doing in their mailbox?"

"I have no idea."

"Are you sure you found a gun in their mailbox?"

"It looked like a gun to me," Cora said. "I suppose we'll have to wait for ballistics."

Bambi looked baffled. "That doesn't make any sense. If the gun had been in the motel room . . ."

"What motel room?" Harper said.

"Didn't she tell you about the motel room?"

"No, she did not. What's this about a motel room?"

Bambi explained how room 106 was right next to Melvin's motel unit. "She searched it first. It was only when she didn't find anything she went looking for this mailbox."

"That's mighty interesting." Harper turned to Cora. "You left that part out of your story."

"When you summarize a case, do you include all the false leads? If I listed every place there *wasn't* a gun, we'd be here all day. I just told you where one *was*."

"So what about the motel room?"

"That was the first theory. It sounded promising, but it wasn't."

"How'd you get into the motel room?"

"Hold on there," Becky said. "My client's not going to say anything about what could possibly be construed as an illegal entry in front of a third party. I'm sure you can appreciate my position."

"I *understand* your position. I don't appreciate it." Harper turned to Bambi. "Besides the motel room number, was there anything that led you to believe there might be anything hidden in the unit?"

"Not really."

"What do you mean, not really?"

"It was just a feeling."

243

"I'll take a feeling. I'll take anything at this point. What was your feeling?"

"Nothing I can point to. Nothing I can put my finger on. It's just, ever since Melvin and I checked into that motel, I've had the feeling we're being watched."

"Is that right?" Harper said.

"Yes. And it's silly, I know. But this guy got killed. And it's nothing to do with us. But he was Melvin's witness. I didn't know him, but I knew *of* him. When someone you know gets killed, it's a little creepy."

"No kidding," Cora said. "So, this feeling you were being watched. That only started after the banker was killed?"

"I don't know."

"I thought you said it was the reason you thought you were being watched."

"I may have had a feeling before and that only made it more so. It's really hard to say when it's only a feeling."

"Well, you be on your guard," Cora said. "As long as we've got a killer on the loose, no one's safe."

Bambi shivered. "Was there anything else?"

"That's all for now. I'll have Dan run you back."

"No need. I brought my car."

After Bambi was gone, Cora said, "Interesting."

"What?" Harper said.

"That she thought she was being watched."

"She *is* being watched."

"That's what's interesting. That she would know it. You gotta wonder how."

"She said it was just a feeling."

"Yeah, but there's gotta be a reason for a feeling."

"Would you know if you were being watched?"

"I've been through four or five divorces, Chief, so that's a rather inappropriate question."

"Four or five?"

Cora shrugged. "You know how it is with husbands. Some die. Some stray. You lose track."

"About this motel room . . ."

"I'm not responsible for what that young thing may have thought."

"Are you responsible for what you did?"

"Of course I am. If I'd actually done anything."

"Did you search that motel room?"

"I've gotta step in here," Becky said. "Unless Cora rented that motel room, which I somehow doubt, I think searching it might technically be construed as illegal."

"Technically?" Harper said.

"See? You won't even grant me that. Come on, Cora. As your attorney, I advise you not to answer any questions about any rooms you might have searched without finding anything until I've had a chance to digest this new information. I'm going to ask you to make no statement whatsoever. It's been nice talking to you, Chief. I'm glad we could help you out, but I'm afraid we must be going."

CHAPTER 37

"You certainly hustled me out of there in a hurry," Cora said.

"No kidding."

"What's the deal?"

"The more this case develops, the more it occurs to me Melvin has fried your brain. Granted, things are coming at you thick and fast, what with another wife besides the one you thought you were dealing with. Even so, we have a bit of a perception gap here. You're slow on the uptake. Which is rubbing off on me, making me slow on the uptake, which I cannot afford to be if I'm your attorney. God knows your attorney must be on the lookout at all times."

"You mind telling me what you're talking about?"

"I'm talking about the Pricherts. The people at one oh six North Street."

"What about 'em?"

"Exactly. Don't you care about them in

the least?"

"Of course not. They have nothing to do with the case."

"That's right. They don't mean a damn thing because you planted the gun in the mailbox. You know it. I know it. But Chief Harper doesn't know it. Under normal circumstances, you would at least *feign* a little interest in the place you supposedly found the gun. But you can't do that. You never even bothered to ask who lived at that address. Chief Harper didn't notice, and God help me, I didn't notice either until Bambi brought it up, which was the right and proper reaction to finding a gun hidden in someone's mailbox. *Whose mailbox was it?* You didn't ask, and when you found out you couldn't have cared less. Ordinarily, you'd never make a bonehead play like that, but with Melvin around, you can't think straight."

"Hey. I can fire you, you know."

"Not a good time in the midst of an alimony hearing. That's for starters. When you've just made your attorney an accessory to a felony, it's a *very* poor time."

"Okay, I won't fire you. But I might rough you up a bit."

"Also considered a poor tactic with litigation pending." Becky shook her head.

"Cora, snap out of it. I need you sharp and focused. We have an advantage over the police because we know where you actually found the gun. Why was it there, and what does it mean? Which is probably the same thing. But at least we can ask those questions. The police can't, which is going to hamper their investigation. So we better come up with something fast, before you're put in the position where you have to confess that the location where the gun was found might not be entirely accurate."

"That would be very messy."

"No kidding. The gun was found next to Melvin's room. A KenKen was slipped under his door, indicating it was there. Does that mean he did it, or does that mean he didn't do it?"

"That means he didn't do it."

Becky threw up her hands in exasperation. "See? You can't think straight. You give me a snap answer just like that."

"I *can* think straight. It's not a snap answer. Melvin may be pond scum, but he's not stupid. He doesn't kill someone and then throw the gun in the motel room next door. I've married men who might do that, but not him. You throw in the fact he's got an insanely jealous woman who's watching him —"

"Or two," Becky muttered.

"What was that?"

"Nothing. Go on."

"It's much more likely he's being deliberately framed."

"You think his wife did it?"

"That's one possibility."

"What's another?"

Cora pursed her lips. "Say you're a lawyer with a limited practice struggling to make ends meet. Perhaps still paying off your college loans."

"Have you been snooping through my mail?"

"Not you, goosey. Melvin's lawyer. What's-his-face. He's handling an alimony dispute. Strictly small potatoes. Say he wound up killing one of the witnesses."

Becky opened her mouth.

Cora put up her hand. "I know, I know. It makes no sense. There can be reasons in play we know nothing about. But take it as a premise: Lawyer kills witness."

"So he frames his client?" Becky said. "I'm already taking it on faith he kills his own witness for no reason, now I'm taking it on faith he frames his own client?"

"Not at all. He's got plenty of motive for that."

"Such as?"

"First off, he doesn't want to get caught. Self-preservation is always a motive. Second, it gets him work. That's where the poor attorney making ends meet comes in. By framing his client, suddenly he's an attorney in a murder case. With a big retainer and the whole schmear. And he'll have a wonderful advantage over the prosecution going in, because he'll know his client isn't guilty. Any theory the prosecution comes up with will be false, so he won't have a hard time poking holes in it."

"You make a strong argument. Maybe I should frame you for a murder rap."

Cora didn't even bother to acknowledge the wisecrack. "And I wouldn't trust that bimbo any farther than I can throw her." She frowned. "Actually, I could probably throw the skinny bitch pretty far. But you know what I mean. Girl comes to me with a KenKen, all doe-eyed and 'What am I to do?' Well, you can let go of someone else's husband for starters."

Becky smiled. "Oh, yeah. You're really over him."

"Shut up."

CHAPTER 38

Early next morning, Cora scrunched down in the front seat of her car and watched the motel with binoculars. She had no idea what she was going to do. Was that just because Melvin was involved? No. It was because nothing made sense of its own accord. It didn't require the return of a former husband clouding her judgment. Not that Melvin was clouding her judgment. Oh, God, what was it that man had?

The door opened and Melvin's wife came out. The current Mrs. Crabtree. Not the prospective Mrs. Crabtree. The potential Mrs. Crabtree. The Bimbo in Waiting. The Tramp Most Likely. No, this was the real McCoy. The scorned woman whom hell hath no fury like.

The woman pushed a zapper and the lights on the car in front of her unit flashed.

Where the hell was she going? Melvin and the bimbo were still in the love nest. At least, as far as Cora knew. What could be urgent enough to drive the stalker from their door?

Mrs. Crabtree came out of the parking lot and headed back toward town.

Cora hung a U-turn and followed.

Mrs. Crabtree parked in front of the library, got out, and crossed the street.

Cora's pulse quickened.

Was she going back to the police station?

No. She went right on by.

And into Cushman's Bake Shop.

Cora face fell.

The woman wasn't hot on the trail of some new indiscretion of her wayward husband. She'd merely been seduced by the lure of the Silver Moon muffins that Mrs. Cushman passed off as her own. Cora had to admit they were damn good. She wished she had one now.

Melvin's wife was out minutes later with a cup of coffee and a pastry bag. She got in her car and drove straight back to the motel.

The car in front of her husband's unit was gone.

Mrs. Crabtree stood staring at the empty parking space.

Cora could understand the woman's frustration. She's gone fifteen minutes and the bird flies the coop. Tough luck, dearie.

That's how it is with surveillance jobs. You sit on a place twenty-four hours, nod off for a moment, and you're screwed. Welcome to the club.

Mrs. Crabtree seemed torn between driving around to look for Melvin, and waiting for him to return. She chose the latter. Her car lights flashed as she zapped it locked. She opened the door to her motel unit and went in.

Cora had had it with surveillance herself. She drove up to the unit, parked beside Mrs. Crabtree's car, and knocked on the door.

There came the sound of footsteps.

The door opened a crack.

A voice said, "Who is it?"

Cora put her shoulder into the door, pushed with all her might.

The door flew open.

Mrs. Crabtree went over backward and wound up in a heap on the floor.

Cora stepped into the unit, slammed the door shut.

"Let's you and me have a little talk."

The woman gaped up at her.

"I know, I know. I should say 'you and I.' After all, I'm the Puzzle Lady. But there's no one here but us chickens. Or is it we chickens? Hell, I don't care. The point is, things are gettin' rough. The question is whether you have the stomach for it."

Melvin's wife struggled to a sitting position. "Get out of here!"

"That's going to be your talking point? Not particularly helpful. So, did you get me a muffin?"

"Huh?"

"I'm partial to the blueberry ginger, but I also like the cranberry scones. Did you get me one at Cushman's Bake Shop?"

"Are you following me?"

"Are you following Melvin?"

"Was he in the bakeshop?"

Cora smiled. "You're quick on your feet. Or should I say, on your bottom? You're not exactly on your feet, are you?"

The woman got to her knees, pushed up off the floor.

"I should warn you," Cora said, "I'm a master of some martial art or other. I can tie you up like a pretzel."

"I don't want to fight you."

"Glad to hear it. I was bluffing. So let's talk. If you're not going to throw me out physically, you don't have much choice."

"Why should I talk to you?"

"We have something in common. Wouldn't you like to compare notes?"

"No, I would not."

"That's understandable. You're still married to the guy. The wounds are fresh. But trust me. I've been there, done that. I could probably help you out."

"What do you want?"

Cora reached in her purse for her cigarettes. "Do you smoke?"

"No."

"Too bad. Anyone married to Melvin should have a hobby." Cora held a match to her cigarette. "Any ashtrays around here?"

"This is a no-smoking room."

"Just my luck." Cora lit her cigarette, pulled over the wastebasket to use as an ashtray.

"Are you always this rude?"

"Absolutely not. When I married Melvin, I was sweet as could be. So, what's your game, sweetie? You getting evidence for a divorce, or you want him back?"

"What makes you think I want him back?"

"So you do. You think you can beat the bimbo's time?"

"Bambi?" She snorted. "The poor girl hasn't got a clue."

"Oh?"

"She's just the flavor of the month. And not even this month, either."

"Really? So who is?"

"You don't know? She testified for him in

court. At least, she tried to."

Cora frowned. "The teller? Melvin hit on the teller?"

"He called on her in the bank and took her out to dinner."

"You're kidding! What did Little Miss Hotpants have to say about that."

"She wasn't here."

"What?"

"She came up and joined him for the hearing."

Cora put up her hand. "Wait a minute. Wait a minute. Melvin came up here first? She came up and joined him?"

"That's right."

"How'd she get here?"

"Huh?"

"If they came up separately, why don't they have two cars?"

"She took a bus."

"Oh?"

"He picked her up in Danbury."

"When?"

"Day before the hearing."

Cora frowned. "I'm confused again. He picked her up the day before the hearing. But she wasn't here when he took the teller to dinner?"

"No, that was last week."

"Last week!"

"Yeah. He came up early to 'check out the witnesses.' He tried to check out Lilly Clemson, all right."

"Melvin's been in town since last week?"

"Yeah."

"How do you know?"

"How do you think?"

Cora frowned. "And all he did was romance the teller?"

"He didn't romance her."

"Whatever you want to call it. That's all he did?"

"He also had a talk with the other witness."

"What other witness?"

"The bank manager who testified."

"The one who got killed?"

"Yeah."

"Melvin had a talk with him?"

"That's right."

Cora had completely forgotten her cigarette. The ash was nearly two inches long. It fell to the floor. "Before or after he had dinner with the teller?"

"Both."

"Huh?"

"He talked to him in the bank. Right after he talked to the teller. He went from her window to his desk. That night he took her to dinner."

"Okay, that's before. You say he also talked to the bank manager after he took the teller to dinner?"

"That's right."

"The next day?"

"No. After he testified."

Cora's mouth fell open. "Melvin talked to the bank manager the same day he testified?"

"You know Melvin. He'd want to review the guy's performance."

"He talked to him right after court?"

"No. He saw him later."

"In the bank?"

"No."

"Where did he see him?"

"In his house."

CHAPTER 39

Melvin's smile was smug. "I knew you'd be back."

"I'm not back. I'm here because you're in trouble and you're too arrogant to know it."

Melvin chuckled. "And you're worried about me. That is so sweet."

Cora flushed. "I'm not worried about you. No, I *am* worried about you. I'm worried you'll get arrested for a crime you didn't do, and the real killer will get away."

"Worried is worried. I think it's sweet."

"Are you forgetting you taught me to shoot?"

"Probably a mistake. But you're the one woman who took a shine to it."

"Where's Lolita?"

Cora had gone straight to Melvin's unit after talking to his wife. She took a perverse pleasure in doing so. The current Mrs. Crabtree didn't dare tag along for fear of letting Melvin know she was there.

"Bambi went shopping. You know women. They like to shop."

"Good. Let's talk turkey. You didn't just get here the day of the trial. You've been around for a while. You took the teller out to dinner, saw the banker in his house. Seeing as how he got killed, that puts you in a rather precarious position."

"How the hell do you know all that?"

Cora shook her head pityingly. "Were you present at our divorce hearing? Our very first one, way back when. All that stuff I had on you. You think I hired a detective to get it? Those guys wanna be paid. The point being I'm pretty good at finding things out. I know you came up here ahead of Bambi, nosed around, made a play for the teller. What in the world were you thinking? I mean, the testimony's ice cold unless you make it look like it's concocted. The only way you can do that is by messing with the witnesses. But you just can't help running your game. You meet a halfway decent woman, you gotta turn on the charm. She buying it, by the way?"

"What do you care?"

"I don't. Except we got a crime that makes no sense, and you managed to stick yourself smack dab in the middle of it. It's a dreadful situation. Left alone, the police will take your actions at face value and arrest you for murder. And guess what? Becky Baldwin can't represent you, she's representing me. Which leaves you with that two-bit ambulance-chasing divorce lawyer, or shelling out an astronomical sum to hire some big-time defense attorney from New York. Either way, I wouldn't like to be you."

"You're crazy."

"Oh, yeah? Ignore what I'm saying, keep on what you're doing, and when they read you your rights, think before you talk."

"You really do care about me."

"I don't want you in jail doing time. I want you footloose and fancy free, chasing women and paying the alimony you're still going to owe me when I win the legal suit."

"What are you talking about? You're using a lot of words to say the simplest thing. That's what you used to do when you were flustered." He grinned. "Not just flustered. Hot and bothered. Remember?"

"No."

Melvin laughed. "Well, there's an overreaction. You're gonna give me one-word answers to prove you're not turned on?"

"You're despicable, you know it."

"Ah. A compromise." Melvin cocked his head. "Wanna grab some lunch?"

"What about Bambi?"

"She can take care of herself."

"I was sure that was your attitude. I just wanted to hear you say it."

"Shall we go?"

"You must be kidding."

"He, I'm a lot of things, but a kidder isn't one of them. You wanna go out with me?"

Cora took a breath. "No, Melvin. I don't want to go out with you. I just want to tell you where you stand. Right now you're an excellent candidate for a murder rap. I just hope they don't arrest you before you lose the alimony suit."

"I'm not going to lose the alimony suit."

"Sure you are. The witness blew up on the stand, couldn't ID the check. I don't think the shyster you hired has the guns to repair the damage."

Melvin scowled. "You let me worry about that."

"I certainly will. Not that it's going to matter. You might as well go home. If you go back to New York before anyone thinks to arrest you, you can fight extradition." Cora's smile was mocking. "If you stall long enough, maybe I can solve the crime before the Connecticut authorities manage to bring you back."

Cora got in the car and drove home. She was angry at herself for letting Melvin get to her. He'd done it so easily, too, with just the slightest innuendo and an offer of lunch. Rattled her completely. Maybe she could solve the crime, hell. Talk about whistling in the dark.

If she couldn't hold herself together any better than this, it would be up to Chief Harper to solve the crime.

CHAPTER 40

The young man looked upset. He also looked familiar. Of course, everyone in Bakerhaven looked familiar. It was a small town. Even so, Chief Harper had trouble keeping them straight. The man looked like an O'Reilly or a Coopersmith, but the chief was damned if he knew which.

"What's the trouble?" Harper said.

The young man shifted from foot to foot. "You can tell, can't you? Boy. I was never good at hiding anything. Take it from Lilly. Sorry, I'm nervous. I'm Luke Haas, Lilly Clemson's boyfriend. Lilly called me last night, all upset. She's a witness and she wasn't very good. Becky got her rattled on the stand. That's Becky Baldwin, Cora Felton's attorney —"

"I know all about it," Harper said. "Go on."

"The man she was testifying for . . ." He grimaced. "That sounds like she was for

265

him. She's not. The guy making all the trouble. Melvin something or other. He wasn't happy with the way she testified. He came to her room last night and told her so. Scared her silly. He didn't mean to. Quite the opposite. All oily and smiley and persuasive. Made her flesh crawl. Anyway, she was scared."

"So she called you."

"Yeah. I tried to get her to go to the police, but she wouldn't do it. And she told me not to say anything. She'd be mad if she knew I was here. If there's any way you can keep me out of it, I'd appreciate it."

"What do you want me to do?"

"Isn't there a law about intimidating a witness?"

"Yes, there is. Who's making that allegation?"

"What?"

"You said keep you out of it. So you're not making the complaint. And the witness isn't making the complaint."

"What about the police?"

"It's not like it's a criminal proceeding. This is a civil suit. A squabble about money."

The young man started to protest.

Harper put up his hand. "Yes, you're still not allowed to intimidate a witness. And,

266

yes, it's a crime. But unless someone is making that allegation . . ."

"Like who?"

Harper hesitated. The obvious "who" was the defendant in the action. But the thought of telling Cora Felton her ex-husband was making trouble was more than he could deal with. "Okay, I'll talk to her. See if she wants to make a complaint."

"You're going to talk to Lilly?"

"Sure."

"Then she'll know I told."

Harper sighed. As if it weren't bad enough having an unsolved murder. "Where does she live?"

"She rents a room. From the Hunters. Paul and Sally. You know them?"

Harper probably knew them on sight. He ignored the question, said, "She has a room in the house?"

"Over the garage, actually. She has her own separate entrance."

"But the garage is near the house?"

"Yes."

"And there's neighbors? People who could have seen this man go in?"

"You mean people who could have reported an intruder?"

"Best I can do for you." Harper picked up the phone, called the First National Bank.

"You'll be discreet?"

"I'm the sole of tact," Harper said dryly. "Hello? Who's this? . . . Oh, hi, Ben. Chief Harper here. Listen, could I speak to Lilly Clemson? . . . She's not?" He glanced at his watch. "What time does she usually get in? . . . Is she often late? . . . I see. Thanks, Ben."

Harper hung up the phone, got to his feet.

"She's not there?"

"No."

"Call her room. I got the number."

Harper called, got no answer.

"What does that mean?"

"I don't know. But I don't like it. Let's take a run over there."

"My car's out front."

"Fine. I'll take mine. You lead the way."

Harper fell in behind Luke Haas, who'd been parked down the block, and drove out to Lilly Clemson's.

He had half a mind to call Cora Felton. One of the witnesses who testified at her hearing was dead. Now the other one was missing. It didn't necessarily mean foul play, but even so it was an ominous coincidence. The only thing that stopped him from calling was the fact that Lilly Clemson *was* a witness in her case. As long as the alimony dispute was pending, Harper didn't want to do anything that might taint the results.

Haas pulled into the driveway of a two-story frame house on the outskirts of town. A separate garage, painted white with green trim to match the house, had a wooden stairway up the side to a platform in front of a doorway in a dormer. It was rather ugly architecturally, but it did create a garretlike artist's residence above the garage.

Harper climbed the stairs with the boyfriend hot on his heels.

There was no doorbell.

Harper pounded on the door.

There was no answer.

"Damn. We'll have to break in."

The boyfriend looked embarrassed. "Um . . ."

"What?"

"I have a key."

"Why didn't you say so? Open the door."

Haas unlocked the door.

Harper pushed it open and stepped inside.

Lilly Clemson lay in the middle of the floor. Her eyes were open and staring. Her throat had been slit. A straight razor lay in the pool of blood that had seeped from the wound.

Luke Haas took one look and gagged.

"Get out!" Harper grabbed the young man, spun him toward the door. "Throw up outside!"

Harper thrust the young man out the door, turned back toward the body.

Sighed.

He wished like hell he'd trusted his instincts and called Cora Felton.

There was a KenKen on the body.

5–	8+		1–	1–	
				30x	
15+		48x			
		11+		2÷	
2–		36x	7+	8+	3
5					

CHAPTER 41

By the time Cora got there, there were two police cars, the medical examiner, an EMT unit, and the Channel 8 van.

Rick Reed pounced as soon as she got out of her car. "I'm talking with Cora Felton, the Puzzle Lady, who has just arrived at the scene of the crime. What can you tell us, Miss Felton? Did the police call you in?"

"Why, did they call you?" Cora said.

Rick Reed, who had been called by Dan Finley, was taken aback. He recovered quickly, said, "Does this mean there's a puzzle involved?"

Cora smiled, pushed on past. She nodded to Sam Brogan, who was handling crowd control and riding herd on Luke Haas.

"Who's he?" Cora said.

Sam popped his gum. "Boyfriend."

Cora ducked under the crime scene ribbon and went up the stairs.

It was crowded in the little room. Barney

271

Nathan was trying to examine the body without kneeling in the blood. The EMT team was at the top of the stairs, waiting to go in.

"What do you want, Chief?"

Harper glanced around. He had no place to pull her aside except for the tiny bathroom. He considered it, shuddered, motioned to her to hang on.

Barney rose from the corpse. "Pretty straightforward. Killer cut her throat. Doesn't appear to be any contributing cause of death."

"When did it happen?"

"Sometime last night."

"Not this morning?" Cora said.

The doctor regarded her with a jaundiced eye. The Puzzle Lady's assessments of his talents had not always been glowing. She might even have hinted at botching an autopsy or two.

"I wasn't aware of your authority to ask questions."

"Consider I'm asking," Harper said.

"It was last night. It could have been the middle of the night, but not as recent as this morning. The blood's coagulated. The body's cooled. It's been a while."

"Was that so hard?" Cora said.

The doctor gave her a look and went out.

The EMT unit came in, fetched the body.

"Okay, Chief. What was it you didn't want to spill in front of them?"

Harper gave her the KenKen.

Cora looked disappointed. "Is that all?"

"Can you solve it?"

"Of course I can solve it. It's not going to mean anything."

"The other one did."

"That was a little different."

"How is it different?"

Cora wasn't sure how to answer that. It was different in that she was *lying* about it, but that wasn't what she wanted to tell him.

"In that case, there was a crossword puzzle involved. Was there one this time?"

"If so, I haven't found it yet."

"Thank goodness."

Chief Harper looked at her. "Why do you say that?"

"Well, the case is confusing enough," Cora said breezily. "So, you want me to take a look at the KenKen?"

"Yeah. I want you to solve it for me and tell me what it means."

"I assume you already added up the numbers in it?"

"Yeah. They come to one eighty-two. Does that suggest anything to you?"

"Not at all."

"I suppose we should check out any address with a one eighty-two in it. One eighty-two Oak Street. One eighty-two Main."

"What in the world for?"

"Well, that's how it worked with the other number puzzle. The KenKen gave you the street number. The crossword puzzle told us what street. In this case, the crossword puzzle is missing. We have to assume we have the street number, we just don't know *which* street. Unless we have the crossword puzzle to narrow it down, we have to check out every address with a one eighty-two in it."

"Oh, for goodness' sakes."

"What's wrong with that?"

"Chief. In the last case, I checked it out, and what did I find? The murder weapon." Cora pointed to the razor on the floor. "Isn't that the murder weapon right there?"

"I would think so."

"So a street address is meaningless. It has to be something else."

"I don't quite follow the logic."

"Trust me, Chief. One eighty-two is not an address. For all we know, one eighty-two doesn't mean anything. The answer could be in the solution to the KenKen."

"How can that be? You told me all Ken-

Kens were the same."

"They all add up to the same number. But the order of numbers is different. Let me solve the thing and see what we've got."

"You can't solve this one. We'll have to make a copy."

"Have Dan run it off."

"Dan's busy."

"With what?"

"We have this murder. Pick it up at the station later."

"You're not going to give it to me?"

"Not the original."

Cora shook her head in exasperation. "Gee, Chief, I'm sure glad you called me down here."

Harper grinned. "A crime scene? You wouldn't have missed it for the world."

CHAPTER 42

Melvin Crabtree walked up the front steps of the police station, cocky, arrogant, head high. From his attitude, he might have been about to receive a medal instead of be arrested for murder.

Rick Reed pushed through the crowd that had formed, stuck a microphone in his face. "Mr. Crabtree, Mr. Crabtree. Is it true you're under arrest for the murder of Lilly Clemson?"

Lennie Fleckstein waved his arms and jumped up and down, as if trying to make up for his diminutive size with an excess of zeal. "No comment! No comment! My client is innocent of these outrageous charges! He is exercising his right to remain silent!"

"Like hell!" Melvin said, pushing his attorney out of the way. "I don't *need* to remain silent. That's what crooks do to avoid getting caught in a lie. I'm innocent, and the truth can't hurt me."

"Did you know Lilly Clemson?" Rick said.

"She was a witness in my divorce hearing."

"Were you at her apartment?"

"At the time of the murder? Most certainly not."

"Were you *ever* at her apartment?"

Fleckstein jumped back in. "Now you are asking questions that have nothing to do with the crime. This is why lawyers advise their clients to remain silent. And why clients have the good sense to follow that advice."

Melvin laughed. "My attorney means well, but he is a little over his head. I did not hire him to battle this ridiculous charge. He is here merely to reduce my alimony payments. If I didn't *have* a lawyer, I wouldn't have *hired* a lawyer, because I don't *need* a lawyer. I'm going to have a little chat with the police now, and see if I can point them in the right direction, because they are obviously clueless."

Smiling and waving, Melvin went in the front door.

Cora watched him go. She was well hidden in the midst of the crowd, so as not to be spotted by Rick Reed. Ordinarily, she would have been all too happy to make a statement, but if Sherry saw her defending

Melvin on TV, she would never hear the end of it.

Not that Melvin needed defending. The idea that he'd killed someone was absurd. In the first place, it was not in his nature. In the second place, it was not in his interest. There was not a chance in hell Melvin had done it, and there was no reason to jump to his defense.

Even so, Cora found herself clenching and unclenching her fists.

In the front of the crowd, obviously equally frustrated, was Bambi, looking particularly doe-eyed and helpless. If she wasn't careful, Rick Reed would pounce on her. Cora wondered if Rick knew who she was. He was an investigative reporter, you'd think that would mean he'd investigate.

As soon as Cora had the thought, the reporter's attention seemed to focus on the bimbo. Of course it could just be because she was young and pretty. Cora grimaced. It really wasn't fair, the whole age advantage thing. Even a mindless twerp like Bambi got such a running start.

Before he reached her, Bambi took a step back into the crowd, leaving Rick with no one to aim his microphone at but Iris Cooper. The selectman was always a good interview, but not what Rick had in mind.

Cora wasn't interested in what her friend had to say. She was interested in finding Chief Harper and asking him politely why he had neglected to mention he was arresting her ex-husband. That small tidbit of information must have slipped his mind.

Cora didn't see the chief, but she spotted a face in the crowd. The current Mrs. Crabtree, she of the clandestine surveillance and perfidious intentions. There she stood, watching her husband hauled off to jail with ill-concealed delight. Cora could empathize with the woman. When she was married to Melvin, there were times she'd felt exactly the same way.

Becky Baldwin fought her way through the crowd, grabbed Cora by the arm. "How the hell did this happen?"

"I have no idea. I was on my way to the police station to pick up a copy of the Ken-Ken, and all hell broke loose."

"What KenKen?"

Cora filled Becky in on her trip to the crime scene.

"Harper was there?"

"Yeah."

"He didn't tell you he was going to arrest Melvin?"

"No, and it's going to cost him."

"Maybe he didn't know at the time."

"Unless he stumbled on a note in the victim's pocket saying, 'Why don't you arrest Melvin?' he knew at the time."

"I see."

"Becky, you've got to defend him."

"What! Are you kidding me?"

"His lawyer's a moron. He can't handle this."

"I can't either. I'm your lawyer. Conflict of interest, remember?"

"I don't think it applies. I mean, *I'm* not suspected of the murder."

"You should be. Every witness who testifies against you gets whacked."

"No one believes that. You should be Melvin's lawyer."

"Why? Why do you want me to?"

"Because I don't know the facts. I'm groping around in the dark. Melvin's been arrested, and I don't know why. If you're his lawyer, you can find out. I need the facts to solve this case."

"Like hell," Becky said.

"Excuse me?"

"As if you couldn't get the facts. Chief Harper's going to be so eager to make it up to you, he'll tell you anything you want. You just want me to protect the guy."

"That's ridiculous."

"Oh, yeah? When there wasn't the slightest chance Melvin was involved, you didn't want me anywhere near him. Now he's in trouble you don't give it a second thought." Becky put up her hand. "Not that I don't need the work, but I don't really want to get a reputation for stealing other lawyers' clients. If you don't mind, I'm sitting this one out."

Before Cora could protest, Becky slipped away in the crowd.

Cora saw Dan Finley coming toward her.

"Dan, what's going on?"

"Got the puzzle for you." He handed her the KenKen.

"Yeah, yeah," Cora said impatiently. "Why did you arrest Melvin?"

"Chief Harper told me to." When Cora started to fly mad, he put up his hands. "Hey, not my fault."

"What do you have on him?"

"You know I can't tell you that."

"Oh, come on. You know Chief Harper will tell me."

"The chief can tell you anything he wants. Because the chief won't get mad at the chief for telling."

"So I won't tell him you told me. Come on, Dan. It's me, Cora. What's the scoop?"

"Oh, hell." Dan glanced around to make sure no one was listening, and filled her in on the boyfriend's account of Melvin's visit to Lilly Clemson.

"So, the chief held out on me," Cora said.

"Yeah, but you can't accuse him of it until you hear it from someone else."

"Where is the chief?"

"Probably still out at the crime scene."

"You going out there?"

Dan shook his head. "No, and neither are you. I gotta run the murder weapon down to the lab. You gotta be a good girl and stay out of trouble." He smiled, headed for his car.

Cora fumed. That was the problem with a small-town police force. With Dan on the way to the lab, Chief Harper at the crime scene, and Sam Brogan on crowd control, there was no one left to bother.

And no one watching the prisoner.

That left him locked up inside. His lawyer was with him, but no police officer.

Cora fumbled in her purse for a cigarette. Came out with her gun. That was an idea. She could shoot her way in and have a talk with Melvin.

Cora stuck the gun back in her purse, pulled out her cigarettes. Looked for a match. Of course she didn't have one. It was that type of day. She glanced around for someone she could ask. No one smoked anymore. Damn. What was the world coming to?

Cora started pulling things out of her purse. The first thing she came up with was her diaphragm. Great. Let's wave that around the crowd a little. Rick Reed can get a shot.

Cora stuck it back, groped some more. What felt like a lighter was only a lipstick. Another thing that felt like a lighter actually was but didn't work.

An oddly shaped object proved to be a string of little firecrackers. She'd picked them up in a novelty shop for far more than they were worth. Probably meant they were illegal. She wasn't up on such ordinances. She shoved them back in the purse, groped some more.

Just as she was cursing her fate, one lone match.

Cora turned her back to the wind, bent over, cupped her hands. Flames shot up toward the cigarette. She sucked in. Yes. No. Yes!

The cigarette caught fire. Cora blew out the match, straightened up, sucked glorious smoke into her lungs. Smiled wryly at the irony of feeling elation at satisfying a disgusting vice. Cora didn't care. She sucked at the nicotine, tried to calm her frazzled nerves.

Tried to think straight. Becky was right, damn it. It was Melvin, and she wasn't thinking straight. Or was it Sherry who'd said that? Or everybody?

Cora looked over at the police station, where Rick Reed was trying to interview Sam Brogan. That would be a fascinating interview. Rick would be lucky if he got anything besides "Yup" or "Un-huh."

Still, it was keeping Sam busy.

Cora walked down the street. Everyone was looking at the police station. No one was looking at her.

Cora crouched behind a parked car, fumbled in her purse again. Pulled out the string of firecrackers. She puffed on the cigarette until it glowed, then held the end to the fuse.

It sputtered, then began sizzling and sending off sparks. That was good. Cora was afraid it was too old. But apparently not. She set the firecrackers on the ground, stood up, walked quickly back to the other side of the crowd, and pushed her way to the front.

Rick Reed was clearly taxing his brain to the limit formulating questions to which

Sam Brogan could answer "Yup" or "Un-huh."

"Did you see the body?" Rick ventured.

The first firecracker went off, then the rest in rapid succession.

People gasped.

Everyone turned, including Sam Brogan and Rick Reed.

Cora went up the steps of the police station and slipped inside.

CHAPTER 43

Melvin was sitting on the narrow cot in the holding cell. His attorney was standing by the bars, trying to reason with him.

Cora sized up the scene, said, "Screw, shyster."

Lennie Fleckstein stared at her. "What?"

"I need to talk to your client. Take a hike."

"Like hell."

"Melvin, tell your mouthpiece to beat it."

Melvin grinned. "You're dating yourself with your gun moll lingo."

"Yeah, yeah. When the first gun was fired, I pulled the trigger. You, wait outside. If a cop comes in, try to head him off, and start talking loud."

"I don't work for you."

"Tell him to get lost, will you? We haven't got much time."

"Beat it, Lennie."

"She's the opposing party," the lawyer protested.

"Not in the murder, she's not. Stop thinking lawsuit. We get me out of jail, *then* we crush her like a bug."

"That's the spirit," Cora said. "Now, get out of here before I throw you out."

Lennie grumbled and stalked out the door.

Melvin was grinning from ear to ear. "Christ, that's how I remember you. What a hellcat!"

"Oh, isn't *that* what every girl loves to hear."

"Come on. It was a perfect match-up. You always gave as good as you got."

"You cheated on the honeymoon."

"You cheated before it."

"I did not."

"You were so drunk you don't remember."

"I remember perfectly. You sneaking out with the floozy."

"I never snuck out. You may have *passed* out."

"You're not endearing yourself, Melvin."

"Oh, no? What are you doing here?"

"Trying to get you out of jail. Before that stupid ambulance chaser gets you convicted."

Melvin shook his head. "Couldn't happen."

"That's what you think. You saw the

victim last night. Cops know it. They're looking to prove it. Bet you a nickel you weren't careful about fingerprints."

"What the hell are you talking about?"

"Don't play dumb. You were unhappy with Lilly Clemson's testimony. Thought she could do better. Tried to threaten and/or seduce it out of her."

"Who told you that?"

"Lilly Clemson. Indirectly. Your charm didn't work on her. She called her boyfriend. Told him what you tried to do. She was very upset."

"She called her boyfriend?"

"Yeah."

"After I left?"

"Yeah."

"That's good."

"How is that good?"

"Proves I left. Right? Dead girls don't make phone calls. The boyfriend proves I left."

"You coulda come back."

"Coulda, woulda, shoulda. All I have to do is prove I left and it doesn't matter how many fingerprints the prosecution throws around." He spread his arms. "I didn't do it." Melvin smiled roguishly. "So, now that that's settled, you wanna catch some dinner?"

"I don't think the preschooler you're dating would like that very much."

"She thinks I'm in jail. We can knock one off before she even knows I'm out."

"You're not out."

"I will be, as soon as you tell the flatfoot about the exonerating phone call. Hell, I should buy the boyfriend a beer. Guy's all broken up, still has time to do me a good turn. Come on, get me outta here, we'll go someplace special. Maybe skip dinner, check into a motel."

"You got a teenage supermodel waiting for you and you wanna take me to a motel?"

"You know how boring young girls are? Aside from the sex, they're no real competition."

"Oh, you smooth talker, you. So you're willing to endure some boring lovemaking in the hope of a stimulating conversation."

Melvin grinned wickedly. "As if you could ever be boring. Before things fell apart, remember how good it was?"

Cora did, just for a second. She hoped it didn't show on her face. Realized it didn't matter. Melvin would catch the hesitation. Melvin always did.

Desperately, she changed the subject. "I don't think you understand. The cops know all about the boyfriend. How do you think they found Lilly to begin with? Boyfriend went to the cops, told them about you. You may think it proves you left, but clearly the cops don't. The boyfriend story is what got you in here."

Melvin's eyes twinkled. "You ran like hell from reminiscing, didn't you? You know what we had. And now look at you. You must have quit drinking. You're sharp. You're focused. Hell, we could take Manhattan."

"Then we'll take Berlin."

"That's right. Hide behind song lyrics. You always were quick with a quote." He smiled at her.

Cora smiled back. "You're married, aren't you?"

The quick change of subject caught him up short. "Now, why would you bring up a thing like that?"

"Shot in the dark," Cora said. "It stands to reason. You were always married. And not to the bimbo, either, that's for sure."

"How can you tell?"

"She's too happy."

"You're quick with the zinger."

"About your wife."

"What about her?"

"So, you *do* have a wife."

"See, now you're bluffing. You *know* I've

got a wife. Your hotpants lawyer would have looked her up."

"She did. You're married. How's your wife figure in all this?"

"She doesn't."

"Oh?"

"Bloom's off the rose. She's filing for divorce."

"How do you know?"

"Huh?"

"If she hasn't filed yet, how do you know?"

"It isn't rocket science. I've been married before, you know."

"Did she tell you she's filing?"

"No. She said she forgives me and we can work things out."

"So?"

"That's a red flag. You hear that, you run like hell."

"But she hasn't made a move yet?"

"Not that I know of. If she's approached an attorney, he hasn't approached me. Why are we talking about my wife? I can't think of a more boring subject."

Cora took a breath. "It wasn't the first time."

Melvin blinked. "What wasn't?"

"Lilly Clemson. It wasn't the first time you'd seen her. You took her out to dinner. Before the trial."

He frowned. "The boyfriend said that."

"What's the matter?"

"Why in the world would the boyfriend say that?"

"Is it true?"

"That's not the point. How would he know?"

"Lilly told him."

"Really? Why would she do that? She might tell him I came by, tried to get her to change her testimony. But take her out? She wouldn't tell him that. Not if she *went*. She'd try to *keep* him from knowing that."

"So, it's true," Cora said.

Melvin grinned wickedly. "What's the matter? You jealous?"

Through the door came the voice of Lennie Fleckstein, talking loudly. "Hey, Chief, where have you been?"

Then Harper's voice: "Where's your client?"

"He's locked up. I meant to ask you, Chief —"

The door was flung open.

Cora smiled. "Come in, Chief. We were just talking about you."

CHAPTER 44

Harper was furious. He slammed the door of his private office, turned to face Cora. "All right, what the hell do you think you're doing?"

"Trying to help you out."

"Oh, sure. Interrogate my prisoner before I get a chance to. Without his lawyer present. How the hell did you manage that?"

"Just asked him to leave."

"Do you know what a mess this could be? Do you realize what Rick Reed could do with that?"

"Don't tell him."

"I'm not amused, Cora."

"I kind of got that. You wanna keep beating me up, or you wanna know what I know?"

"What's that?"

"Melvin didn't do it."

"Oh, great," Harper said sarcastically. "The guy bats his eyes at you and suddenly

293

he's innocent. What the hell has that creep got that women turn to jelly?"

"I'm not turning to jelly. I'm trying to help you out. If you don't appreciate it, I'll shut up and you can solve your own damn case, but I happen to have the goods."

"Oh, yeah?"

"Yeah. I'm sorry that Melvin happens to be innocent if it makes you so angry. But the facts are the facts. You wanna hear 'em, or you wanna complain you don't like the way they add up?"

Harper took a deep breath. Exhaled. "Fine. What are the facts? *Why* is Melvin innocent?"

"Largely because he didn't do it. But that's not what you mean. You mean, how do I *know* that he's innocent? Melvin points to the fact Lilly Clemson told the boyfriend about his visit. On the theory she couldn't do it if she was dead. It's a poor defense. Of course, he could have come back. But here's the thing. Melvin doesn't know his wife's in town."

"You asked him?"

"Of course not. Then he'd know his wife's in town. I asked him about his marriage. As far as he knows, his wife is at home plotting things with lawyers, or preparing to plot things with lawyers, or whatever. He has no idea she's here. But she is, and if she followed him at night to a young lady's apartment, she might think the worst, and if she was a jealous, vindictive sort, she just might take it out on the woman in question."

Harper snorted in disgust. "So, that's your reasonable doubt. I suppose you suggested this to Melvin's attorney."

"Then they'd know she's in town. They don't know, and let's keep it that way. Until such time as you arrest her for the murder, or pin the crime on someone else."

"I'm still waiting for your proof that Melvin didn't do it."

"I gave you a logical inference."

"I don't want a logical inference. You said you had proof."

"How about this. Melvin left Lilly alive. That's attested to by Lilly's boyfriend. Melvin went back to the motel, where Bambi will swear he never left again."

"Her testimony's worthless. She'd swear that in any case."

"Uncontested, it gets him off."

"That's the prosecutor's problem, not mine."

"It is when Ratface wants to know why you arrested a suspect he can't convict, and demands you do better."

"He's the best I've got."

"That isn't even halfway true. You got Mrs. Melvin. You don't like the jealousy bit? The fact she's here at all proves it."

"She's getting evidence for a divorce, not knocking off his girlfriends."

"What about the boyfriend? Melvin calls on his girlfriend, and what does he do? Go over and make sure she's all right? No, he goes to the police. Makes a complaint. Gets you to go. Why? Because he doesn't want to be the one to find the body."

"What a minute, wait a minute. You're saying the boyfriend killed her?"

"He's more likely than Melvin."

"Why?"

Cora threw up her hands. "It's like talking to a wall. Melvin had no motive. So she didn't do great in court. The punishment for that is death?"

"You make it sound ridiculous."

"Because it *is* ridiculous."

"Is it any more ridiculous than the theory her boyfriend killed her because a guy threatened her for the way she testified in his divorce hearing?"

"Not when she went out to dinner with him." Cora frowned. "Do I mean 'Not when'? This is too long and convoluted a dialogue chain. I'm not sure if the negative is correct here. Or do I mean to say 'It is when'?"

"What the hell are you talking about?"

"Linguistics. Never mind. The point is, Melvin took Lilly out to dinner. Before she testified."

"You know that for a fact?"

"Yeah."

"Why didn't you tell me?"

"Because I know the way your mind works. The more Melvin was involved with her, the more reason he'd have to kill her. Which isn't true. The more Melvin was involved with her, the more reason *her boyfriend* would have to kill her."

"He didn't do it."

"How do you know?"

"He went to pieces when he saw her."

"Of course he went to pieces. Her throat had been cut."

"It wouldn't be a shock if he'd done it."

"Sure it would. Take a killer, throw his murder in his face. You think he wouldn't react?"

"Crabtree still looks good for it. You throw in he went out with the girl —"

Cora inquired if Chief Harper was an amorous individual of limited intelligence.

The chief was shocked. "Cora!"

"Every time I think you're getting better you disappoint me. So Melvin killed both of his witnesses against me in the alimony hearing? How the hell does that make any sense?"

"We didn't arrest him for both crimes. Just the one."

"Do you think someone else did the other? And they both just happened to leave Ken-Kens with the bodies? Two separate serial killers armed with number puzzles?"

"If they each did only one, they're not serial killers."

"No. They're copycat killers. It's a fraternity stunt. Everyone has to commit a similar crime."

"Speaking of number puzzles . . ."

Cora groaned. "For Christ's sake."

"Have you solved it yet?"

"Dan just gave it to me."

"Right. You had no time to solve it. You were too busy interviewing my prisoner."

"I'll be happy to solve it, but it's not going to mean a thing."

"Is that a professional opinion or just an educated guess?"

"I'm not sure it's educated."

"Come on, Cora. You gonna help me or not?"

"I've *been* helping you. I've been doing nothing *but* helping you. Not that you seem to notice."

"Come on. Solve the damn thing."

Cora sat down, whizzed through the puzzle.

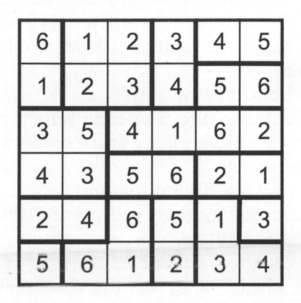

6	1	2	3	4	5
1	2	3	4	5	6
3	5	4	1	6	2
4	3	5	6	2	1
2	4	6	5	1	3
5	6	1	2	3	4

"There you go."

"So what does it mean?"

"I have no idea, without a clue to point me in the right direction."

"The other one pointed you to a mailbox with a gun."

"That one didn't come with a corpse. It came after the murder."

"Yeah. And guess who it was delivered to? The gentleman currently in jail."

"You keep coming back to Melvin."

"No, the *clues* keep coming back to Melvin. I'm just following the clues." Harper pointed to the KenKen. "So tell me, what is there about this number puzzle that points to Melvin that you don't want me to know?"

"You think it's his cell phone number? Too short. The number of women he's been with might be about right, but how would anybody know?"

"You're just being silly."

"The idea is silly. Someone puts a cryptic clue in a KenKen puzzle and expects anyone to figure it out."

"And yet you found the gun."

"There was a crossword puzzle. Find me a crossword puzzle."

"As a matter of fact . . ."

Cora's heart sank. Was the chief really going to throw a crossword puzzle in her lap, expect her to solve it on the spot? How was she going to tap-dance her way out of that?

"As a matter of fact what?" Cora said irritably.

"I was just going to ask you if perhaps there had been a crossword puzzle from some other source."

Cora's heart fluttered and she sucked in her breath. Just the type of guilty reaction a cop would be apt to notice. Why was he asking her that?

"You're asking if someone sent *me* a crossword puzzle that would explain what this KenKen means?"

"I was not asking specifically if anyone *sent* it to you. I was asking if you got one from any other source. Like filched it from the crime scene before the cops could get a look."

"I wasn't *at* the crime scene."

"Yes, you were. I saw you there."

"That was after you'd been there and searched it. You think I stole something from the crime scene you missed?"

"I don't know what you're capable of these days. Your ex-husband comes to town and you start acting different. I don't know what you're capable of."

"I'm not capable of finding something that isn't there."

"Not when I saw you. But had you been there earlier, before the cops? In time to spirit the evidence away?"

"Would that be a felony?"

"It certainly would."

"Then I couldn't possibly have done it. I'm a law-abiding citizen."

"If that turns out to be the case . . ."

"It won't. Because I didn't do it. This KenKen is as meaningless to me as it is to you. And I have no idea, whatsoever, of anything that might shed any light on it. Including, but not limited to, anything I might have found, seen, or heard of that could possibly relate to this jumble of numbers at all."

"You're really worked up, you know."

"Oh, right," Cora said. "Pester and goad me until I react and then tell me I'm really worked up."

Harper nodded sympathetically. "I can make allowances. I understand how you feel. I'm sorry I arrested your man."

Cora's face reddened. Her eyes blazed.

"He's not my man!"

CHAPTER 45

"Sherry. Thank goodness you're home."

"Of course I'm home. You've got the car."

"Oh, that's right."

"Where are you calling from?"

"Pay phone at the Country Kitchen."

"You gotta get a cell phone, Cora."

"Yeah, yeah. Look. You gotta do me a favor."

"What?"

"Run down to the mailbox."

"Why?"

"See if anyone sent us a puzzle."

"What makes you think they would?"

"There was a puzzle when the banker got killed."

"That led us to your license plate. I thought you weren't admitting that."

"I'm not."

"You think there's a puzzle this time?"

"I don't know."

"Implicating you?"

"Or Melvin."

"You're worried about Melvin."

"Give it a rest, Sherry."

"That's so cute."

Cora started a string of invectives, but Sherry had put down the phone. The screen door slammed as she went out.

Sherry was back minutes later. "Nothing there."

"Good."

"Why is that good? Couldn't you use a hint just now?"

"A hint would be fine. A crossword puzzle would be embarrassing. Since I just swore up and down to Chief Harper there wasn't one."

"Oh, here's Aaron. Hey, honey, in the kitchen! Maybe he's got something."

"If he did, he wouldn't be home."

"Hi, honey," Aaron said. "Is that Cora?"

"Yeah."

"Good. Lemme talk to her." Aaron's voice came over the phone. "Cora, I got something for you."

"What?"

"The boyfriend. He went ballistic when he heard Randolph asked her out."

"How do you know?"

"I'm a reporter. That's my job."

"How come you didn't get it before?"

"The boyfriend wasn't important before. The fact Randolph asked Lilly Clemson out wasn't even news until Rick Reed started touting it. The word now is the boyfriend had a fight with the banker."

"Physical or verbal?"

"Word is just verbal, but plenty heated."

"I see."

"I thought you'd be more pleased."

"Why?"

"It lets Melvin off the hook."

"I'm not in this to get Melvin off. I'm in this to find out what actually happened."

"Right," Aaron said.

He didn't sound convinced.

CHAPTER 46

"Becky! You gotta help me!"

Becky Baldwin looked up from her desk. "Christ, I wish you had a cell phone."

"I'm glad I don't. My life is complicated enough without it."

"Yes. But then your lawyer can't reach you. I need Chief Harper to butt out of my business. He was in here reading me the riot act. You snuck into the holding cell and interviewed his prisoner."

"I wasn't *in* the holding cell."

"Oh. Touchy. He didn't say it was a conjugal visit. He said you had a talk."

"Why was he telling you?"

"I'm a licensed attorney. I have to cooperate with the law."

"You're a licensed attorney and you have to respect the confidence of your client."

"Thank you. I needed that refresher course in legal ethics. The problem is, Harper thinks you're holding out on him."

"I *am* holding out on him."

"What?"

Cora grimaced. "You're gonna beat me up, but there was no reason to tell you. Now there is. Harper thinks maybe I found and suppressed a crossword puzzle that would tie in the KenKen found with Lilly Clemson's body. I didn't, but I did in Roger Randolph's murder."

"What?"

Cora told Becky about finding the crossword puzzle and having it yield her own license plate number.

"You held out on me?" Becky said.

"Well, it hardly seemed relevant to an alimony hearing."

"Did it seem relevant to the murder?"

"I wasn't charged with the murder."

"Even so."

"Even so? I don't believe that's a valid legal argument. Sway many judges with the phrase *even so?*"

"The thing is, that only makes it worse."

"What?"

"Your position."

"I don't have a position. I didn't do it. I may be involved in manipulating the location of the murder weapon, but that's hardly the same thing. And completely unrelated."

"That must be one of the most extraordinary statements between a client and her attorney. Let me be sure I understand you

307

correctly. Your suppressing of and tamper-ing with evidence in a murder is entirely coincidental and not to be inferred."

"Exactly. Couldn't have said it better my-self."

"I was being sarcastic."

"I noticed. So why were you so eager to get in touch with me? Just to bawl me out?"

Becky exhaled, grimaced. "We have a problem. It was a problem before you told me about Chief Harper, and it's a bigger problem now."

"What are you talking about? You said you *saw* Chief Harper."

"Yeah. But he didn't tell me what you said."

"What I said about what?"

"About denying there was a crossword puzzle."

"So? That's not your fault. You didn't know he asked me. You didn't know I told him. You're not responsible for any mislead-ing statement you may have made while speaking in ignorance of the facts."

"Right. That would be a sin of commis-sion. As opposed to a sin of omission."

"It's not a sin if you didn't know it. And why the hell are we talking sins? This is not a religious matter, it's a legal matter. You did not legally withhold anything by failing to mention what you didn't know." Cora shook her head in exasperation. "It's a sad reflection on the legal profession when you have to educate your own lawyer."

"I didn't know he was going to ask you that specific question. It puts me in a hell of a position."

"Why?"

Becky opened her desk drawer, took out a folded document, passed it over.

Cora opened it up.

It was a crossword puzzle.

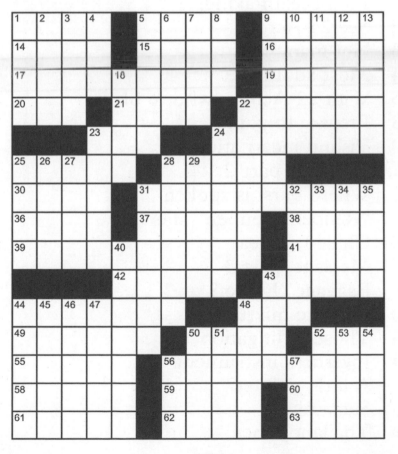

ACROSS

1   Money owed
5   Large-scale
9   Serious accident
14 Vicinity
15 Facial tissue additive
16 "Whole _____ Shakin' Goin' On"
17 Message, part 1
19 Made waves?
20 WJM-TV anchor
21 Find breathtaking?
22 See 25-Across
23 Not many
24 Most adoring
25 With 22-Across, who to blame
28 Prepare to paint
30 Vishnu incarnation
31 Message, part 2
36 Where Farsi is spoken
37 "Reuben, Reuben" star
38 Chilled, as tea
39 Message, part 3
41 Baggage checker?
42 Metallic mixture
43 Those in litigation
44 Inverness instrument
48 A little pointer?
49 Sans injury
50 Thailand, once

52 "Yo!"
55 Get up
56 Message, part 4
58 Thin, as sound
59 Oodles
60 Vaccine type
61 Belgian violinist/composer
62 Auberjonois of "Star Trek: Deep
    Space Nine"
63 In the pink

DOWN

1   Bonkers
2   Eastern lake, canal, or city
3   Relax, as rules
4   Smidge
5   Colorful squawker
6   Shakespeare title starter
7   Thick fog, in slang
8   "Get it?"
9   "Up in the Air" star George
10 Author Dahl
11 Based on _____ story
12 Petunia propper-uppers
13 Lacked, briefly
18 Improved, as wine
22 Red, to a red baiter
23 Old French coin
24 Foul-mouthed

25 Barbershop request
26 _____-kiri
27 "_____ my wit's end!"
28 Magazine about celebs
29 Reached in amount
31 Make a bust?
32 Arrange a date for
33 Subdivision unit
34 Eye drop
35 Ben & Jerry's competitor
40 Clairol colorer
43 Water collector
44 Buxom
45 Those opposed
46 Accra's land
47 Producing groans, maybe
48 Cut's partner
50 Mall event
51 Pressing need
52 Also-ran of fable
53 And more, for short
54 Cheerleader's bit
56 Jam ingredient?
57 Despondent

CHAPTER 47

Cora let go of the puzzle as if it were hot. The paper fluttered down, landed on Becky's desk.

"What the hell is that?" Cora demanded.

"It's a crossword puzzle."

"I can see that. Why do you have it, and why are you giving it to me?"

"It was shoved under my door. I had it when I talked to Chief Harper. At the time, I had no idea he'd asked you if you'd seen such a document and that you'd denied it existed. That makes you technically innocent of lying to the police on that particular subject, and makes me technically innocent of compounding a felony and conspiring to conceal a crime. Because I wasn't asked the question directly and you weren't aware of the puzzle's existence when you spoke to the police. We are both technically innocent. And if you think that is going to get us off the hook when it turns out you *were* withholding a similar crossword puzzle with regard to the *other* murder, we're screwed six ways from Sunday."

"Yes and no."

"Yes and no? I've already granted all our technical defenses. Aside from that, how does this strike you as a yes-and-no situation?"

"The puzzle only becomes a problem if the police know about it."

"Oh, my God," Becky said. "Now we both know about the puzzle's existence. We both know it's been demanded by Chief Harper. And now you're suggesting we suppress it while in full knowledge of the facts."

"Well, when you put it like *that* . . ."

"Cora." Becky shook her head ruefully. "The only way out of this mess is for me to contact Chief Harper immediately. Tell him that you've apprised me of the fact he's looking for a crossword puzzle to go with the KenKen that was found at the scene of the crime. That I had previously received a crossword puzzle slipped under my door. That I had no idea what it was until I heard from you. That the minute I did I immediately contacted him and turned it over."

"Works for me," Cora said.

Becky frowned, looked at her. "What do

you mean, it works for you? Then the chief has the evidence and we don't have any idea what it is."

"Well, I assume he'll give us a copy to play with."

"You think so? After we held out on him?"

"We didn't hold out on him. At least, not this."

"Yeah. You know it and I know it. You think the chief is going to believe it? We'll be lucky if he lets us see it at all."

"He's going to want it solved."

"Yeah, but not by you. Hasn't Harvey Beerbaum been helping him out with puzzles lately?"

"Only with things that don't matter. Harvey can solve the puzzles just fine, but he can't figure out what they mean."

"That's all well and good. But I'm not giving it to Chief Harper without you solving it first."

"He's not going to like that."

"He's going to love it. We're giving him the puzzle and the solution without him having to ask."

"It's not a good idea."

"Why not?"

"You said so yourself. *You* held out on the chief. *I* held out on the chief. But we didn't know it. We got together and realized we were doing it. So what did we do? Give him the puzzle? No, we solved it to make sure there wasn't anything incriminating in it."

"That's not what we're doing."

"That's what it will look like."

"Of course it will look like that. Because that's exactly what we're doing. Don't you want to know what the puzzle says?"

"How could it possibly help?"

"I don't know, because I don't know what the puzzle says. But I sure as hell intend to. So, you want me to act as your lawyer, you tell me what the damn thing says."

Cora heaved a deep sigh. "Aw, hell." She picked up the phone, punched in the number. "Sherry? Aaron still there? . . . No, I don't want to talk to him. I'm at Becky Baldwin's office. Get him off his duff and get him to drive you down here just as fast as he can."

CHAPTER 48

Becky couldn't believe it. "You can't do crossword puzzles?"

"Number puzzles I can do just fine. Crossword puzzles drive me nuts. When Sherry and Aaron were on their honeymoon, I had Harvey Beerbaum solve the puzzles for me."

"You're kidding."

"I had to tell him. He wasn't shocked. He said a lot of constructors can't solve puzzles."

"And that's you?"

"I can't solve worth a damn."

"Will you guys shut up?" Sherry said. "I'm working here."

"Oh, look at that," Cora said. "She gets to flaunt her expertise, and suddenly she's a diva."

"You want me to solve this or not?"

"Well, I'd like to know if it's about me."

"Why would it be about you?" Becky said.

"It wouldn't," Cora said. She hoped it was true.

"Maybe it *is* about you," Sherry said. "24 Down is 'Foul-mouthed.' "

"Is the answer 'Cora'?" Becky said.

"No, but it's six letters starting with F. Could be 'Felton.' "

"If you fudge the answer to spell Felton, I am *so* going to get you," Cora said.

"Like I'd do that."

"I don't know *what* you'd do," Cora said. "You've been acting so erratic lately."

"What do you mean, lately?" Becky said.

"Ask Mom and Pop."

"Mom and Pop? I knew you were building an addition, but —"

"Done!" Sherry said.

"What is it?" Cora said.

"See for yourself."

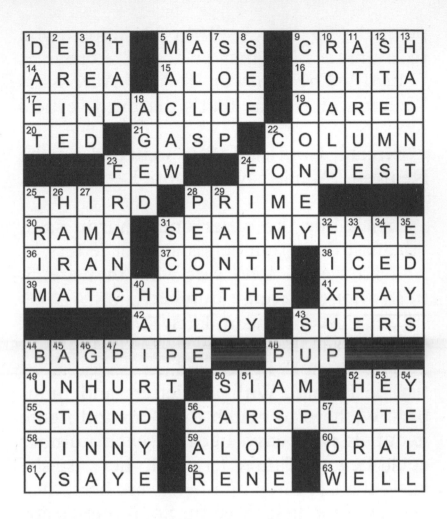

Cora grabbed the puzzle, read: " 'Find a clue. Seal my fate. Match up the car's plate.' " She snorted. "Yesterday's news. We matched up the car's plate. It points to me."

"Not necessarily. You've got another Ken-Ken."

"Right. So what am I supposed to do? Look at the second row across?"

"No." Sherry took the puzzle back. She

pointed. "25 Across. 'With 22-Across, who to blame.' The answer to 25 Across is 'Third.' The answer to 22 Across is 'Column.' I assume that's the third vertical row."

"Great," Cora said. She snatched up the KenKen. "What have we got? Let's see. '2, 3, 4, 5, 6, 1.' "

"If it's like the other one," Aaron said, "the first three numbers stand for letters."

"Yeah, well, I don't care what they are, 5, 6, 1 is not my license number."

"Let's see whose it is," Aaron said. "Lemme see the phone."

"The phone?" Becky said.

"The keypad. With the letters and numbers. We have to match them up and figure it out. It isn't easy, because each number could be any of three letters. In her case she knew the last three numbers were hers, then we saw if the first three fit. So, if there's any license plate that has these last three numbers —"

"Hell!" Cora said.

"What is it?" Sherry said.

"I know whose plate this is. I was driving around looking for it. It's Melvin's."

CHAPTER 49

"Okay, what do we do now?" Cora said.

"There's no what-do-we-do-now," Becky said. "What we do now is turn this over to the police."

"We can't give the chief another lead to Melvin. It'll practically ice the case."

"Oh, come on," Aaron said. "No one's going to find him guilty on account of a crossword puzzle."

"It's not a question of finding him guilty. It's a question of holding him in jail. Making statements to the press. Giving interviews to Rick Reed. Can't you see it now? PUZZLE LADY'S EX IMPLICATED IN MURDER BY PUZZLE. Hell, people will think *I* did it."

"Hey, there's a thought," Aaron said. "You wouldn't be trying to get back at him for the alimony suit, would you?"

"Of course she isn't," Sherry said irritably.

"Think about it, Aaron. Just how likely is that?"

"I'm not saying she did. I'm just saying it's a tough theory to disprove. I mean, you give the police a crossword that implicates Melvin, there's only two things they're going to think. One, it implicates Melvin. Or two, you're trying to implicate Melvin. Particularly when you're the one giving it to the police."

"I wasn't the one who found the damn thing," Cora said.

"No, your lawyer was. How much weight is that going to carry? You say, 'No, I didn't find it, my lawyer did.' "

"Sherry, you married a real pain in the ass."

"He's just telling you what the cops are going to think. And it *is* what the cops are going to think. Don't lay it on him. Hell, even *I* have trouble with the story someone gave this to Becky."

"Oh, you think I made it up?"

"No. But maybe someone gave it to you, and Becky's covering for you. So no one will get the *idea* you made it up."

"Oh, my God," Becky said, "no one squabbles like relatives. What is this, "Dysfunctional Family Feud"? And it's a moot argument. The puzzle was given to me. I'm giving it to the cops. End of story."

"Yeah, but it's not the end of the story," Cora said. "Because then they're going to want to know what it means."

"Why? It's solved."

"Yeah. And you think that will satisfy Chief Harper? He's going to want to know what the solution means."

"And you tell him it's referring to a license plate. Not that big a jump from 'car's plate.' "

"Then he's going to want to know whose plate."

"And you'll tell him you don't know. You don't, do you? I mean, you haven't matched it up."

"Well, not entirely."

"Okay," Becky said. "First off, let's clear the room. I need to have a confidential conversation with my client. You guys gotta go. Before you do, I need to know. Are you going to talk to the police?"

"Now, hang on," Aaron said. "It depends what you mean by *talk*. I'm a reporter. I have to follow the story."

"That's not what I mean, and you know it. Are you going to blab to the police about the crossword puzzle?"

"Not unless directly asked."

"And you're not going to do anything that

would *lead* them to directly ask. You're not gonna write this."

"Come on, Becky," Sherry said. "You know he won't write it."

"Unless I get it *from* the police. Which is something else entirely."

"And then you'll be circumspect?"

"I was born circumspect."

Becky turned on Cora. "All right. If you keep your mouth shut, are they going to come up with Melvin's plate?"

"I don't know."

"Well, how could they? Aside from trial and error. They won't have letters, just numbers."

"Yeah," Cora said doubtfully.

"What's the matter?"

"When I came up with my plate, two things happened. First of all, I knew it. Aaron came up with the idea of using the telephone keypad. He was trying to figure out what letters the numbers would stand for. I recognized the last three numbers of my plate. Then we checked the others."

"The police may not think to use a telephone keypad."

"Maybe not. But when I figured it out we didn't know we were looking for a license number. They will. 'Find a clue. Seal my fate. Match up the car's plate.' "

"So they'll check Melvin's plate because he's a suspect."

"It's a little worse than that."

"How can it be worse than that?" Becky said.

"When I spotted Melvin in court I had Dan Finley check around, see if he'd rented a car. Dan gave me the plate. Not only does he know the number, he knows *I* know the number. So, if the plate does happen to match . . ."

"Does it?"

"It sure looked like the last three numbers. If it is, it's gonna be pretty bad."

Becky looked at Cora in disgust. "And that's without the first crossword puzzle that points to your license number."

"Yeah. Which is too bad, because if the cops knew there was one implicating me, they'd be less apt to think I was behind it."

"Now you want to confess to withholding evidence to put your actions in a better light."

"Isn't that what you're doing with the puzzle you got?"

"I am turning over that puzzle to the cops at the earliest opportunity after I realized it was important."

"Wouldn't that opportunity have come and gone?" Cora said.

"No one's holding a stopwatch on me. I got it today. When did you get your puzzle?"

"I don't remember."

"Was it today?"

"Oh, all right," Cora said. "Call Chief Harper. Turn over the damn puzzle. And let's put our heads together and see if we can figure out a way out of this damn mess."

CHAPTER 50

Cora and Becky sat at a table in the coffee shop in the mall.

"Why are we at Starbucks?" Becky said.

"Don't be silly," Cora said. "The police want to talk to me. I'm not ready to talk yet. Besides, I need a Frappuccino."

Becky grimaced at the immense frozen concoction in front of Cora. "How can you drink that?"

"With a straw. Sip your skim latte and feel virtuous. I need a treat. It can't hurt. Hell, it might help."

"What is there to help? You've messed everything up. In your insane desire to protect the man who ruined your life. Your least favorite husband, if I remember correctly. The one you wanted to squash like a bug."

"Yeah, him," Cora said. "I'm not going nuts to protect him. But he didn't do it. Which means someone else is running

327

around killing people. Do you really have a problem with the fact I'd like that person stopped?"

"I have a problem with the fact you're willing to risk *fine and imprisonment* to have that person stopped. Not that you don't take shortcuts with the law. But this is a little much, even for you. Aside from the crossword you're withholding, there's the murder weapon you pocketed and then planted."

"I didn't pocket it, I put it in my purse."

"It's not funny, Cora. I would like to keep you out of jail. I would like to keep *me* out of jail."

"Believe it or not, I have no problem with that. I would just like to catch a killer, too. Not to mention win the alimony suit."

"I almost forgot about that," Becky said.

"I wouldn't worry about it. If we stall long enough, the killer will knock off all of Melvin's witnesses."

Becky studied Cora's face. "You're loopier than usual. I don't know whether Melvin blew your mind, or if you're just scared and whistling in the dark. Consider this. How would you feel if you lost your career? If you couldn't be the Puzzle Lady anymore?"

Cora choked on her Frappuccino. Had Becky made the connection? Harvey Beerbaum hadn't when she'd told him she couldn't solve puzzles. It never occurred to him she couldn't construct them, either. But Becky had a legal mind. She was used to asking probing questions. Uncovering secrets. Recognizing lies. If she couldn't be the Puzzle Lady anymore? What else could it mean than being exposed as a fraud?

Cora gagged into her napkin, tears in her eyes.

"Are you all right?" Becky said.

"Brain freeze. Ignore it. I'm fine."

"Glad to hear it. I'm not," Becky said. "If you couldn't be the Puzzle Lady anymore, it would destroy you. You would have no column, no career, no TV ads. But that's not going to happen. If you can just stay out of jail, you'll be fine."

Becky pointed to herself. "I won't. I don't have to go to jail to lose it all. I have never been so close in my life to getting disbarred. It's a tough thing to have on your résumé. A bit of a career killer, you know what I mean?"

Cora dabbed her mouth with her napkin, tried to hide the relief she felt at not having been found out. "Look, kid. I'm with you. No one's getting disbarred here. All we have to do is solve this thing. Granted, you've been led into some questionable practices by an irresponsible client. If the police found out, that would be bad. So let's make sure they don't. The quickest way is to solve these crimes so they stop looking."

"When you put it that way, it sounds so easy."

"Hey, this is not rocket science. We happen to know Melvin called on Lilly Clemson last night after previously taking her to dinner. Hell hath no fury like a woman scorned. If a woman he dumped was the jealous type, she just might take her rival out. Does that sound like anyone you know?"

"Yeah, you."

Cora shot Becky a dirty look. "And you give *me* grief for fooling around. I was referring to the current Mrs. Crabtree, who has been secretly spying on her husband, and was not happy he took Lilly Clemson out to dinner. And that was before hubby went to see her in the wee hours of the morning. If you want a killer all gift-wrapped with a nice little bow, she's it."

"She killed Lilly Clemson?"

"Why not?"

"And left a crossword puzzle and a Ken-Ken pointing to her husband?"

"Absolutely."

"Why would she do that?"

"To pay him back for the grief he's given her."

"Yeah," Becky said dubiously. "But if she loves him and wants him back, why is she sending him to jail for murder?"

"She's not sending him to jail. She's giving him grief. The same way he gave her grief. She's leaving just enough evidence to implicate him in the crime, but not enough to convict him. If it did look like the cops had him, I bet she's got some backup plan to put in effect to prove he's innocent. One that wouldn't blow her cover by involving her."

"So she planted the gun in the motel room?"

"Absolutely."

"And sent the puzzles to Melvin and the bimbo?"

"Sure. Knowing they'd bring 'em to me."

"How could she be sure of that?"

"Because they couldn't solve them themselves."

"That's a bit of a stretch."

"A stretch? Are you kidding me? You got a whack job running around killing people and leaving puzzles. Anything she does is going to be a stretch."

"She also killed the banker?"

"Sure."

"Why?"

"To make trouble for the two people she hated most. Melvin and me. She kills Melvin's witness. The one he's taken such great pains to cultivate. She leaves the KenKen to make sure the police will bring me in. Just in case they don't, she diabolically leaves a crossword puzzle at my house. A puzzle implicating me. How embarrassing will that be, when I solve it for the police? Or, what a horrible position I'll be in if I *withhold* it from the police. Which is what she's really hoping for. What a position of power that will put her in. I'm walking around with a bombshell she could explode at any moment."

"How?"

"An anonymous tip. Or another puzzle made public that I *have* to solve. I don't know. The point is, it's the type of thing that sends me to jail and gets you disbarred."

"Keep your voice down."

"It's a win-win for Mrs. Melvin. Particularly if it has the side effect of freaking out the bimbo, who couldn't have had a murder rap in mind when she signed on for the Melvin experience."

"You're serious?"

"You're damn right I'm serious. Someone

killed these people. It wasn't Melvin, but it was someone with an ax to grind, and she tops the list. She's been here from the beginning. She followed Melvin up here, set up shop in the motel, monitored his actions. Saw him meet with the banker, take the teller out to dinner. She didn't like it, but she didn't want to show her hand, so she sent him a little warning by breaking into the banker's house. She didn't take anything, but left a KenKen. Which just happened to yield the amount of the alimony payment we were fighting over. She figured I'd solve it, see the amount, and freak out. It didn't occur to her I'd be too dumb to notice, and wouldn't have known at all if you hadn't pointed it out."

"And why did she kill the banker?"

"First warning didn't take. After court, while you were romancing the lawyer, I bet you Melvin tried to take the teller to lunch. At least dropped by the bank to go over her testimony one more time. Bad move. Mrs. Melvin is pissed. So she strikes. She doesn't want to kill the teller, who hasn't testified yet. She wants Melvin to win the alimony suit. Keep the money in the family. She kills the banker, and leaves a puzzle pointing to me. What she *hadn't* planned on was I've got an ace attorney smart enough to get the banker's testimony thrown out of court. If she'd known that she wouldn't have done it, but she didn't, so she did."

"My head's hurting."

"Have some Frappuccino."

"No thanks. So, she didn't count on the banker's testimony being thrown out?"

"Of course not. Never occurred to her. Hell, never occurred to the *judge,* until you brought it up."

Becky thought that over. "Okay, say she did it. How do we interest the police? With Melvin in jail, they're not going to be very receptive to any theory about anyone else. So how do we drag her into this?"

"Well, we still have a court hearing, don't we?"

"Yeah. So?"

"Call her as a witness."

CHAPTER 51

"Do you trust me, Melvin?"

"What kind of question is that?"

"It's the kind of question a woman asks when a man is in jail and she's not."

Melvin exhaled, gripped the bars of his cell. "Fine. You got the upper hand. Too bad you had to get me arrested to do it."

"I didn't get you arrested."

"No, you just gave the police a number puzzle that happens to have my license plate."

"I didn't give it to the police. It was found at the scene of the crime."

"Lennie said you gave it to the police."

"Who?"

"My lawyer."

"That was a crossword puzzle. And I didn't give it to the police, my lawyer did."

"Your lawyer's trying to frame me? And she seemed like such a nice girl. Hell, I'd fire Lennie if I thought she'd take the case."

"She can't take the case. She's representing me."

"In the alimony hearing. Which is kind of on hold until I get out."

"That's what I want to talk to you about."

"Getting out?"

"No, the alimony hearing."

"Oh, come on, Cora. That's conniving, even for you. What's the deal, I drop my suit and you get me out?"

"I hadn't thought of it, but that's a great idea."

"You're kidding."

"Yes, I am. Did it ever occur to you I want to help you out of the goodness of my heart?"

"For old times' sake?"

Cora grimaced. "Oh, you had to spoil it. Bringing up old times."

"It's not like there weren't any good ones. Remember the boat ride?"

"What boat ride?"

"The gondola."

"That was a rowboat."

"So you *do* remember. You brought a picnic lunch. We spread out a blanket on the shore. That was a nice day. You were happy then."

"I was," Cora admitted. "You know why it was so good?"

"Why?"

"You were married to someone else."

Melvin sighed. "You had to spoil it."

"I'm not here to reminisce. I've got a proposal for you."

"A proposal?"

"Wrong choice of words. I'd say proposition, but that would be worse."

"Not necessarily."

Cora felt that hot rush she used to get way back when. Damn. Melvin still had it. "I need you to focus."

He grinned. "Remember when I had that camera and —"

"Shut up, or I'll get your attorney back in here."

"Not that. I'll be good."

"Okay, here's the deal. The alimony hearing is scheduled to resume tomorrow. I have it on good authority Judge Hobbs is prepared to grant you a continuance on the grounds it would be prejudicial to proceed while you're incarcerated."

"No kidding. So?"

"I want you to reject the offer."

"What?"

"Decline the continuance. Tell him you don't need an adjournment, you're quite prepared to proceed."

"I'm *not* prepared to proceed. Numbnuts

337

out there is so freaked by the murder charge, he's ready to let the case drop. Two of my witnesses are dead. Thanks to your pretty little lawyer, the testimony left in the record isn't nearly enough to prove the case."

"How about your handwriting expert? Can't he swear I signed the check?"

"I don't think that's enough to sway the judge."

"Maybe not, but it's enough he won't grant summary judgment. Becky will have to put on a case."

"Wonderful. Much as I like to see her strut her stuff in her little lawyer getup, I'm kind of distracted by this murder charge."

"This is your best chance of getting off."

"You're kidding."

"Not at all. Play it the way I told you, I think it will be fine. Can you do that?"

"Why?"

"I can't tell you why."

"You're saying something's gonna happen in court?"

"That's right."

"Aside from the alimony? You mean about the murder case?"

"That's what I mean."

"Well, what is it?"

"I can't tell you that. But it's a good bet.

You always were a gambler, Melvin. Whaddya say? Wanna take a shot?"

Melvin studied her face. It had matured since he'd known her, but there was a familiar light in her eyes.

"Okay. I'm in."

"Fine," Cora said. "Now, there's just one more thing."

"What's that?"

"There's something you need to know."

CHAPTER 52

Judge Hobbs was in unusually good spirits. He surveyed the crowded courtroom and said wryly, "I don't know why you're all here." He glanced at the plaintiff's table, where Melvin Crabtree sat shackled under police guard. "I plan to grant the plaintiff a reasonable continuance, adjourn the hearing, and go and play golf."

Becky Baldwin rose to her feet. "We object to a continuance, Your Honor."

Judge Hobbs chuckled. "Nothing to object to, yet. I just told you what I'm going to do. The plaintiff is yet to make a motion. When he does, you can object to it."

Lennie Fleckstein got to his feet. He glanced at his client for reassurance. Melvin looked at him in exasperation, nodded, and gestured for him to go on. The little lawyer turned back to the judge. "Your Honor, we're not asking for a continuance. The plaintiff is prepared to proceed."

Judge Hobbs was flabbergasted. "But, but," he stammered, "you just lost another witness. One whose direct testimony was seriously undermined and which you will not have an opportunity to repair. The mere fact you can't conduct redirect examination seriously hamstrings your case."

"I hope your remarks don't indicate you have a predetermined verdict. It's somewhat singular to have the judge comment on the evidence before it's all in. The plaintiff is ready to go. Unless the defense needs time to prepare."

"The defense is ready, Your Honor."

Judge Hobbs scowled. He motioned the bailiff over. "Call Pine Ridge Golf Course, tell them to hold my tee time. It shouldn't be a problem for them. Half the golfers in town are here."

The judge turned back to the lawyer. "Fine. Call your next witness."

"Call Shelby Whitherspoon."

An angular gentleman with white hair and bifocals took the stand and was sworn in.

"Mr. Whitherspoon, what is your occupation?"

"I'm an examiner of questioned documents."

"Stipulate his qualifications subject to cross-examination," Becky Baldwin said.

341

"Mr. Whitherspoon, I hand you a document marked for identification as Plaintiff's Exhibit Number One, and ask you if you recognize it."

"Yes, I do."

"What do you recognize it to be?"

"It is a check from the estate of Chester T. Markowitz made out to and endorsed by Cora Felton Markowitz."

"Have you seen that check before?"

"Yes. I was given that check and asked to compare it with another check on the account of Cora Felton, made out to cash and signed by Cora Felton."

"And what did you conclude?"

"Aside from the name Markowitz, the signatures are identical."

"I ask that the check, Plaintiff's Exhibit Number One, be introduced into evidence."

"Now just a minute," Judge Hobbs said. "That check was already stricken from the evidence when the witness, Lilly Clemson, was unable to identify it as the one having been given to her by the defendant, Cora Felton. The fact a handwriting expert says it's her signature doesn't prove it's the same check."

"We're not introducing it as the same check, Your Honor. Merely as a check made out to Cora Felton Markowitz which she endorsed. After all, that's the only issue here. Whether the defendant acknowledged herself to be Mrs. Markowitz."

"Thank you for educating me on the law," Judge Hobbs said tartly. "But that does not happen to be the only issue here. The check may be introduced as the one examined by Mr. Whitherspoon, but that's all."

"Thank you, Your Honor. No further questions."

Becky smiled. "In the interest of expediting your golf date, Your Honor, I have no questions."

"Call your next witness."

"The plaintiff rests, Your Honor."

"Very well," Judge Hobbs said dryly. "Tempting as it is to dismiss the suit and play golf, I must reluctantly conclude that granting every favorable inference to the plaintiff, there is sufficient grounds to proceed. Does the defense wish to call a witness?"

"We do, Your Honor."

"I assume that would be the defendant. I should warn you, I am well aware of your client's penchant for flashy, unconventional, outrageous, theatrical courtroom behavior. I tell you in advance any such spectacle shall be grounds for contempt of court."

"Thank you, Your Honor," Cora said.

Judge Hobbs blinked. "Thank you?"

"For the warning. I would hate to be thrown in jail without a warning. It wouldn't seem fair."

The judge opened his mouth, closed it again. "And I will thank you to speak through your attorney. Ms. Baldwin, would you instruct your client that any communications with the court should be made through you?"

"Absolutely, Your Honor. Cora, behave. Let me do the talking."

"Okay. I'll be good."

"Call your witness."

"Call Mrs. Evelyn Crabtree."

Melvin's wife, who had been sitting in the back of the court, got up and came down the aisle. Melvin took it in stride, but Bambi, seated behind him at the rail, was clearly surprised and outraged. She leaned over and jabbed Melvin in the arm. Cora could see her mouthing, "What the hell?"

Mrs. Crabtree made quite a show marching to the stand, what with her flaming red hair and flashing green eyes. She was dressed in a black sheath dress that must have taken a good two weeks of dieting just to get into. She sat on the witness stand and smiled at Melvin, a mongoose hypnotizing a snake.

"What is your name?"

"Evelyn Crabtree."

"Are you related to the plaintiff?"

"He's my husband."

"Now, just a minute," Judge Hobbs said. "Mr. Crabtree, are you okay with the defendant calling your wife to testify against you?"

"Yes, Your Honor."

"Well, I like that," Cora said. "He gets to talk and I don't?"

Judge Hobbs banged the gavel. "Miss Felton, he was asked a direct question by the court. You were not. If you are asked a direct question by the court, you may speak. But if not, the next time you do it is going to cost you money." The judge, badly discomfited, turned back to the plaintiff. "Now then, you may have no problem with your wife's testifying, but I do. I fail to see the relevance it has on whether Miss Felton was married to Mr. Markowitz."

"Surely the marital status of the opposing parties is relevant to an alimony hearing," Becky said.

"I fail to see how."

"Nonetheless, there has been no objection."

Judge Hobbs scowled. "Very well. Proceed."

"Mrs. Crabtree?" Becky said.

"Yes."

"You are married to the plaintiff?"

"That's right."

"How long have you been married to the plaintiff?"

"About a year."

"When you met the plaintiff, was he married or single?"

"He was married."

"To the defendant, Cora Felton?"

"No. To another woman."

"He subsequently divorced her and married you?"

"Yes, he did."

"Now then, were you aware he was attempting to have his alimony reduced?"

"Yes, I was."

"And that he came here for that purpose?"

"That's right."

"And when he came here, did you follow him?"

"Just a moment," Judge Hobbs said. "Relevance?"

"It goes to bias, Your Honor."

"Bias? What bias? The witness seems to be giving her testimony frankly and freely."

"Appearances can be deceiving, Your Honor. I would rather prove a lack of bias than assume it. But I assure you the question is material."

"In what way?"

"In a way that will become immediately apparent as I continue. However, an explanation would be unwieldy, so let's just assume I'm showing bias."

Judge Hobbs pointed at Cora Felton. "Did *she* tell you to say that?"

"Naturally, I discussed the case with my client," Becky said suavely.

"Very well. Proceed. But please get to the point."

"Certainly. Perhaps if we could continue until there's an objection by the *plaintiff* . . . ?"

Judge Hobbs sucked in his breath. Debated whether a reprimand was in order. "Proceed," he said tersely.

"And what did you do?"

"Melvin registered at the Oakwood Motel. I registered in another unit from which I could observe his actions."

"What did he do?"

"He went to the bank, talked to the people who were going to be witnesses."

"The banker and the teller? Roger Randolph and Lilly Clemson?"

"That's right."

"The witnesses who were killed."

"Yes."

"He spoke to them at the bank?"

"That's right."

"When was this?"

"Last week. He came up Wednesday morning to check out the witnesses."

"That's when he saw them in the bank?"

"Yes."

"Is that the only place he saw them."

"No."

"Really? Where else?"

"He took Lilly Clemson out to dinner."

"When?"

"Later that night."

"Where did they go?"

"To the Country Kitchen."

"Did he meet her there?"

"No. He picked her up at her place."

"And drove her home after dinner?"

"Yes."

"Did he go inside?"

"No. But they sat in the car for a while. Probably trying to talk her into inviting him up."

"That's speculative, and will go out," Judge Hobbs said. "I realize there's no objection from the plaintiff, but please try to keep the questioning within legal bounds."

"Yes, Your Honor." Becky turned back to the witness. "Did he *ever* go inside?"

"Miss Baldwin."

"It's not speculation, Your Honor. I'm asking if she knows for a fact."

"Yes, he did."

"How do you know?"

"I saw him."

"You followed him to her apartment and watched him go inside?"

"That's right."

"When was that?"

"The night she got killed."

CHAPTER 53

By the time Judge Hobbs got done pounding the courtroom to order, all dreams of playing golf had vanished in the mist. "Excuse me, but did you just say you saw the plaintiff go into the decedent's apartment on the night of the murder?"

"That's right."

"Mr. Fleckstein, stand up! Counselor, I offered you a continuance on the grounds that your client's arrest on suspicion of murder might have a negative influence on the outcome of this hearing. It never occurred to me this hearing might have a negative influence on the outcome of your murder case. It now appears that it does. If it should turn out that in any way, you have conspired to poison the jury pool and prove that your client cannot get a fair trial, I would consider that to be tantamount to the type of questionable ethics that might be of interest to the bar association. This

woman is the wife of the defendant. Under ordinary circumstances, she would not be allowed to testify against him at the trial. If by allowing her to testify here and 'inadvertently' let slip damaging evidence against him in his murder case, you hope to get such evidence excluded at his trial, and hope to exclude any other evidence the prosecution might hope to introduce as fruit of the poisonous tree, it would be a very serious matter."

"That was not my intention, Your Honor."

"Well, I'd sure like to know what your intention was. Because I can't think of one that could possibly be construed as legal."

"Yes, Your Honor. I should point out, Your Honor, that at the moment the witness's statement stands uncontested. I have the right to cross-examine."

"Not yet, you don't," Becky said. "I haven't finished my direct examination."

Judge Hobbs glowered. "Approach the bench."

Cora got up and started to follow Becky.

"Not *you*," Judge Hobbs said. "The attorneys."

Cora tugged at Becky's sleeve. "Could I make a statement?"

"My client would like to make a statement, Your Honor."

"Well, I don't wish to hear from her."

"Very well, Your Honor. But I should point out, we seem to have arrived at a legal impasse. Perhaps the suggestion of a layperson might help."

"Very well. But be brief."

Cora got to her feet. She leaned back to Becky and whispered, "Call me a layperson again and I'll bop you one. You see that smirk on Melvin's face?"

Cora stepped forward, addressed the judge. "Your Honor, much as I'd like to win this suit — and believe me, I would — I don't want to do it by convicting my ex-husband of a murder he didn't commit. I assure you we don't plan to introduce any evidence that would do that."

"Your bland assurance is laughable in light of the testimony of the witness."

"That's because you haven't heard all of the testimony. I know what she's going to say, and it isn't going to hurt Melvin at all. At least in terms of the murder. I plan to win this case. So, you let her talk, Melvin goes free, and I get my money. It's a win-win. Sure, he loses his money. But under the circumstances, it's still a win."

"And just what is this woman going to tell us?"

"I'd rather you heard it from her. If you

want, I'll ask her questions. If you don't, I'll feed them to my lawyer, and she'll ask them, but it will take twice as long."

Judge Hobbs sighed. All hope of maintaining order in the courtroom and preventing a sideshow had long since gone by the board. "Very well. Make your case."

CHAPTER 54

Cora Felton stepped out in the middle of the courtroom. She smiled at the Channel 8 TV camera for the benefit of the Granville Grains publicity department and Judge Hobbs's skyrocketing blood pressure. She shot a glance at the plaintiff's table. Melvin was grinning from ear to ear. He had a lovely smile, one of his more endearing qualities, and a wicked grin. She remembered the latter more fondly, perhaps because it was more likely sincere. In any event, it was clear her ex-husband was getting a huge kick out of the proceedings. After all, it wasn't every day a man got to see his ex-wife grill his wife on the witness stand.

"Mrs. Crabtree," Cora said, "I'm sorry to put you through this. It must be quite an ordeal. I'll try to make it easy. You are the current Mrs. Melvin Crabtree?"

"That's right."

"How long did you say you've been married to the plaintiff?"

"About a year."

"When did things go bad?"

"Is this relevant?" Judge Hobbs said.

"That's the thing about question and answer," Cora said. "Some answers are more relevant than others. And you never know until you ask the questions."

Judge Hobbs took a breath. "Proceed."

"When did things go bad?"

"Right after the honeymoon."

"You were lucky. Mine went bad *on* the honeymoon." Cora caught the look in Judge Hobbs's eye and said, "But to move along. What went wrong with the marriage?"

"I found out Melvin was involved with someone else."

"Would that be the young lady sitting behind him in court?"

"No. There was another one before her."

"What happened to her?"

"She dropped him like a hot potato when she found out he was married."

"What happened then?"

"He took up with Bambi. That's the young woman sitting there."

"Did she mind he was married?"

"No."

"How do you know she knew?"

"I made sure she knew."

"How did you do that?"

"I sent her a little note."

"You didn't accost her in person?"

"No."

"Why not?"

"I wasn't sure I could control myself."

"Interesting. You're afraid of losing your temper where your husband's transgressions are involved?"

"Weren't you?"

"Yes. But I had an advantage. Melvin taught me to shoot a gun. Big mistake on his part. I was damn good, and he knew it. You never want to cross an angry woman with a gun." Cora smiled, leaned in confidentially. "So, I'm wondering if Melvin learned from his mistake."

"What do you mean?"

"Did he teach *you* to shoot?"

"I don't see how that's relevant."

"So he did. You happen to own a gun?"

"No, I do not."

"If you do, it's easy enough to prove. They have to be registered, there are licenses involved. Which means you don't have a legal gun. It is my understanding from friends in the police department that the gun that killed Roger Randolph was an unlicensed gun, an illegal gun, stolen from a sporting goods store. If that were your gun, there would be no record."

The witness said nothing.

"Is that your gun?"

"No, it is not."

"Going back to your surveillance of the plaintiff. You set up shop at the same motel as the plaintiff, followed him around. You saw him take the witness Lilly Clemson out to dinner."

"That's right."

"Did he also take the witness Roger Randolph out to dinner?"

"Of course not."

"Why?"

"He's a man."

"So the only conversation he had with Roger Randolph was a week ago Wednesday afternoon when he called on him in the bank?"

"No. He also called on him in his house."

There was a rumbling in the court.

Judge Hobbs banged the gavel.

"Now," Cora said, "if we could avoid another outburst, since Judge Hobbs is rather touchy today, could you try to soft-pedal the fact it was the night Randolph died?"

Despite Cora's admonition, there were gasps in the court.

"Is that right?" Judge Hobbs said ominously.

"Yes, it is, Your Honor. But we really shouldn't be making such a big deal of it. People call on people. People die. It's not necessarily cause and effect." Cora turned back to the witness. "In any case, you saw him go into Randolph's house on the night of the murder?"

"That's right."

"And you saw him go into Lilly Clemson's apartment on the night of her murder?"

"That's right."

"In both cases he was there."

"Yes, he was."

"And so were you."

"Huh?"

"You were there. At the scene of the crime. On the night of both murders."

"What are you implying?"

"I'm not implying anything. I'm just asking questions. As the judge pointed out, some of them are more relevant than others. Do you do KenKen?"

The change of subject was so abrupt, the witness blinked. "What?"

"KenKen. The new number puzzles. They're all the rage. They even have them in *The New York Times,* right next to the crossword puzzles. Can you do them?"

"Why?"

"Interesting response. Implies you do. If you didn't, you'd say no."

"Yes, I can do puzzles. I still don't know why you're asking."

"Because puzzles were found at the scene of the crime. Pointing to Melvin's guilt." Cora frowned, shook her head, deploring. "Which bothers me greatly. I have yet to hear an adequate explanation for why a murderer would leave puzzles at the scene of the crime that pointed to himself as the killer. It's really only the sort of thing someone would do if they wanted to *frame* someone for a crime. Which still doesn't work for me, because it's such a clumsy frame. However, aside from the puzzles at the crime scenes, there are also the puzzles slipped under the door of Melvin and Bambi's room at the motel. Seeing as how you're staying at the same motel, I'd be hard-pressed to think of anyone with a better opportunity to do that."

"I didn't."

"Yeah, but your denial is a self-serving declaration, of no evidentiary value. You'd need an independent witness to establish you didn't do it. Anyway, the puzzles laid on Melvin and Bambi led to the recovery of the gun. And not just any gun, but one which I understand ballistics proved conclusively was the gun that killed banker Roger Randolph."

Mrs. Crabtree said nothing. She sat tight-lipped, glowered at Cora.

"Do you have a laptop?"

"Why?"

"Once again!" Cora said. "No wonder Melvin couldn't stand you. Your evasions are so transparent. I'm going to assume your answer was yes, and I'm going to tell you why. If you did compose those puzzles, I'm assuming you had Crossword Compiler on your machine. You composed them on your laptop, hooked up to a printer, and printed them out. If those puzzles are on your laptop, you're a dead duck."

"I have a laptop. The puzzles aren't on it."

"I didn't think they were. Anyone smart enough to have thought up this whole scheme would be smart enough to destroy the evidence. I'm assuming you deleted the puzzles and uninstalled Crossword Compiler. Which would be enough to thwart me. Or Chief Harper. Or even the guys at the crime lab. Well, bad news for you. I got a gang of computer nerds standing by who can find things on your laptop even after you delete them. So, where's your laptop? In your car?"

"No. It's in my motel room."

"Your Honor, I suggest the court stand in recess long enough to allow Chief Harper to escort the witness out to the Oakwood Motel and take possession of the laptop computer she has there."

Judge Hobbs blinked. "For what reason? This is not a murder trial. This is an alimony hearing."

"All right, so let me put it another way. We've been going at this for a long time now. What do you say we take a little break?"

Judge Hobbs looked over to where Chief Harper was conferring with District Attorney Henry Firth. The prosecutor caught the judge's eye with a stern look that made his case more eloquently than any summation.

"Very well," Judge Hobbs said. "Court will stand in recess for one hour."

CHAPTER 55

Chief Harper was taking no chances. He
didn't follow Evelyn Crabtree back to the
motel, he drove her there in his police car.
He pulled up in front of her unit and was
right behind her when she opened the door.

"Okay, where is it?"

She pointed to the desk. "There."

"Is it plugged in?"

"No, it's charged."

"Good."

Harper reached in his back pocket, pulled
out an evidence bag. He unfolded it and,
touching the computer only with his hand-
kerchief, maneuvered it into the bag.

"Is that really necessary?" Mrs. Crabtree
said.

"I have no idea. But if I don't do it, some
smart lawyer will ask me why I didn't."

"There's nothing on it."

"Then you have nothing to worry about."

"You don't know Melvin."

Harper ushered her out of the motel room, put the evidence in the back of the cruiser. "You ride up front."

"I rode up front on the way over."

"And you're riding up front again. On the way over, there was no evidence in the backseat you might want to tamper with."

Harper pulled out of the motel parking lot and headed back to town.

Cora Felton and Dan Finley watched them go. They were in Cora's convertible, parked just out of sight around the bend.

"I don't know what I'm doing here," Dan said.

"I'm paying you back for getting me that car rental plate."

"By making me sit here for an hour when I could be having coffee and a scone?"

"I'd like one, too. We didn't have time to stop."

"Why not?"

"We wouldn't be able to swear the chief took the witness back to the motel."

"I would think the chief would be capable of establishing that himself. Or do you think he needs corroboration? Is the woman apt to lie?"

Cora sighed. "Any woman married to Melvin is apt to lie. Ah, here's someone."

A car pulled into the motel parking lot.

"That rental plate look familiar?"

"It's Melvin's."

"Yeah. Since he's in jail, I think we can assume it's the bimbo. Sure seems in a hurry, doesn't she?"

"Well, she's only got an hour. Probably going to change into another outfit."

"Why, Dan Finley," Cora said. "Been noticing the young strumpet, have you? Well, she's closer your age than Melvin's."

Dan was blushing splendidly. "I assure you, I was only —"

"Keep it. Here she comes again. . . . Uh-oh, she's turning this way."

"Think she'll see us?"

"If you keep your head down, she may think it's just a parked car."

Bambi didn't see them. She zoomed on by, rocketed down the road.

"Okay, flatfoot," Cora said. "Here we go. If we get stopped, you pay the fines."

"What?"

"You really gotta get a sense of humor, Dan. It'll help you with the girls."

The rental car flashed around a turn a couple of hundred yards ahead. Cora stomped on the accelerator, shot down the road like a NASCAR driver heading for the flag. She screeched through the turn and straightened up just in time to see Bambi's

car zoom out of sight up ahead. She tromped down harder on the accelerator.

"Are you crazy!" Dan said. "Slow down."

"Sorry. This is a Toyota. They don't stop."

Half a mile ahead, the brake lights flashed and the car turned right. Cora made up the distance, fishtailed through the turn.

The rental car pulled up alongside the riverbank. Bambi jumped out. She had something in her hand.

"Okay, kid, you're up. Got your handcuffs ready?"

Cora screeched to a stop in the gravel. She wrenched the door open and jumped out. "Don't do it, Bambi!"

Bambi stood frozen. A deer in the headlights.

In her hand was a laptop computer.

CHAPTER 56

Chief Harper was somewhat perplexed. "You take a recess to collect evidence against one person, and arrest another?"

"Yeah," Cora said. "Isn't that nice?"

"The prosecutor doesn't think so. Now he's got two people arrested for the crime."

"Yeah, but he's going to let Melvin go."

"I'm not so sure."

"I am. For one thing, he's innocent. For another, if he holds him, he can't hold the person who actually committed the crime. Both seem like excellent reasons for letting him go."

"Assuming they're true."

"You know they're true. Just look at the little hussy. Did you ever see a more guilty-looking woman?"

"Yeah, but she won't talk. She asked for a lawyer and clammed."

"What more proof do you need?"

Harper looked at her in exasperation.

"How can you say that? You're always haranguing me about defendants' rights, and how stupid cops are for taking silence as an indication of guilt."

"Yeah, when they're innocent. Then it's really stupid. But when you've got some bimbo who's guilty as sin . . . Hell, the way she *moves her hips* is an indication of guilt."

"I'm not sure you're entirely rational on the point."

"You're the one not being rational, Chief. You got her laptop. She was apprehended trying to destroy it. You're probably going to find the puzzles on it. Or at least the programs to create them."

"Can you tell me what happened? In simple, plain English I can pass on to the district attorney?"

"I'll use words of one syllable."

Chief Harper gave her a dirty look.

"I'll be good," Cora said. "Here's the dope. My ex-husband, Melvin, is a low-life, philandering creep."

"You seemed quite close to him."

"You wanna hear this or not?"

"Go on."

"His wife, the redhead spitfire, doesn't take it lying down. She fixates on him with the type of obsessive hatred only guys of his caliber can inspire."

367

Harper raised his eyebrows.

Cora put up her finger. "I warned you."

"I'm listening. I'm listening."

"She pesters his girlfriend with the usual tactics. Did-you-know-he's-married notes, stuff of that ilk. She spies on him, keeps a record of his indiscretions. They play the game. Melvin tries to hide stuff from her. She tries to find out.

"What he doesn't try to hide is his alimony scheme. He's always short of money. His excuse is the alimony he's paying. The reality is the bimbo he's banging. Anyway, my monthly bill is something he and the current Mrs. Melvin can agree on. Both would love to see it stopped.

"And so it comes to pass that Melvin has to go to Bakerhaven. It's a business trip, he's going with his lawyer, his wife can't come. Of course, he's *going* with his lawyer, but he's not *staying* with his lawyer, because he's going to be joined by the young and nubile Bambi.

"Here's where the whole thing bites him in the ass, and you'll pardon me a bit if I gloat. He's cheating on his wife with his current girlfriend, but it doesn't mean he's dead. He tells *Bambi* it's a business trip and she's gotta stay behind, at least until he gets everything set for the hearing. It's partly true; he is lining the witnesses up. But he also wants to get away from his current squeeze and check out the other fish in the sea.

"Lilly Clemson is female, and she has a pulse. Just Melvin's type. He makes a play for her. Big mistake. The wide-eyed, innocent Bambi is actually a cold, calculating schemer.

"Bambi rents a car and follows. To see if Melvin is cheating on her. And what does she find? It's a parade! Melvin's being followed by his wife. Bambi spots Mrs. Melvin, but Mrs. Melvin doesn't spot her. She probably plotzed when the woman turned into the same motel. What the hell! Was Melvin cheating on her with his own wife?

"But, no, Mrs. Melvin rents a unit, watches her husband from a distance. Bambi watches both of them. When Melvin goes out, he's got a double tail. The redhead and the bimbo. Hmm. Sounds like a TV show. Bet I could pitch that.

"Melvin makes a play for the teller. Takes her to dinner, tries to talk his way upstairs. He's spied on by his wife and his girlfriend.

"His wife is merely amused. This is the type of behavior she's grown accustomed to from the philandering son of a bitch. But the bimbo is royally pissed, decides to fire a warning shot across the bow. Without revealing her presence, of course.

"Bambi's a whiz at puzzles. What can I tell you, some airheads are. She composes a simple KenKen. Breaks into the banker's house and leaves it there."

"In his *safe?*" Harper said. "How the hell did she get into his safe? Don't tell me she's a safecracker, too."

"It was probably unlocked. She was trying to make the room look like it had been searched. She took the picture down off the wall, found the safe. It was unlocked because there was nothing in it. Perfect. She pulls the door open, puts the KenKen in.

"And what was the point of the KenKen? To attract yours truly. The former Mrs. Melvin. The last link in the chain. Past, present, and future. He must have talked about me. She must have hated me as much as the current Mrs. M.

"Anyway, she left the KenKen. When you solve it, the top line gives you the amount of my alimony payment."

"What?!"

"Didn't I mention that?"

"You certainly didn't."

"Well, it didn't mean anything to anyone but me."

"It *would* have meant something to me if

you'd *told* me."

"Let's not get off on a tangent. The point is, it's a clue. Whoever composed the Ken-Ken knew the amount of my alimony payment. Bambi wanted Melvin to get out of paying me alimony so he could spend the money on her. So Bambi would know. She put the amount in just to goad me."

"When did you know this?"

Cora smiled. "Lets not start worrying about who knew what when. This isn't the Watergate hearings."

Harper scowled.

Cora pushed on quickly. "Which brings us to the first day in court. The banker testifies. I'm a little put off by the fact the guy who's testifying against me is the same guy whose robbery I was just investigating. It's a coincidence, and I don't like coincidences, and I'm right, because it actually *isn't*.

"Anyway, the banker testifies, and we break for lunch. Bambi's back at the motel — at least, that's what Melvin thinks — so he tries to take the teller out to lunch. A bad move, but then in Melvin's case there've been so many. He makes another play for the teller, displeasing both wife and mistress. Some more than others.

"Bambi, born with a homicidal streak, might have offed the teller. But she hasn't

371

testified yet. And it is in her interests as Melvin's girl that he stop shelling out money to me. No such problem with whackin' the banker. He's already testified. Or so Bambi thinks. She can't have anticipated Becky will be smart enough to get the testimony thrown out. She goes off and composes the KenKen and the crossword puzzle."

"Crossword puzzle? What crossword puzzle?"

"Oh. Didn't I mention the crossword puzzle? This is a confusing case, Chief. So many things to keep straight."

"There was no crossword puzzle found with Roger Randolph. Just a KenKen."

"Right. The crossword puzzle came to my house. So it had nothing to do with the KenKen. It's just a coincidence they were connected."

"Really?" Harper said, suspiciously. "What did the crossword puzzle say?"

"Oh."

"What was it?"

" 'Being a bad boy in court cut his life very short.' "

"You didn't think that was connected to the crime?" Chief Harper said sarcastically.

"Not unless you think *I* did it. *I* don't think I did it. So how could it possibly apply?"

372

"I don't know. But don't you think that should be up to the police to determine?"

"Absolutely. What do *you* think it means, Chief?"

"Don't get smart with me. You're getting in deeper every minute."

"Don't be silly, Chief. We're solving the crime. All of this is just incidental. You wanna hear the rest of it, or you wanna beat me up?"

Chief Harper took a deep breath, exhaled very slowly. "Go on."

"So, Bambi offs the banker. With the gun she had hidden in her car."

"Car? What car?"

"Now that's something you can check, Chief. She came up here last Wednesday. Most likely in a rental car. Drove around in it until Sunday when it was time for Melvin to pick her up at the bus stop. Then she beat it down to Danbury so she could pretend she'd just arrived. Her rental car's gotta be parked somewhere near the motel so she could follow Melvin when he took off in his."

"She committed the other murder, too?"

"Of course she did. Once Lilly Clemson testified, she was dead meat. Bambi had to use a razor because she'd already ditched the gun. She slit her throat, left the puzzles implicating Melvin."

"The KenKen gave us his license plate."

"I know."

"She tried to get him convicted?"

Cora shook her head. "Of course not. She loves him. No, like I said in court, implicating Melvin doesn't implicate Melvin. Not unless you think Melvin's stupid enough to implicate himself, and trust me, he isn't dumb. Bambi knows the current Mrs. Melvin is on the scene following hubby around. Bambi's trying to make it look like his wife is framing him."

"I don't know."

"I do. That was her plan from the start. If there's anyone Bambi hates worse than me, it's the current Mrs. M. For Bambi it's a situation made in heaven. All she has to do is leave a few clues around. If she can make it look like Melvin's being framed, Evelyn Crabtree sticks out like a sore thumb. The only problem is no one knows she's there. Her husband hasn't spotted her, and no one knows she's Melvin's wife. That's why she tried to give us a hint."

"Who tried to give us a hint?"

"Bambi. When Dan brought her to the police station. She tells us she's got this funny feeling she's being watched. What she's really saying is, 'Hey, dumb-dumbs, there's a woman with hair as red as a Raggedy Ann doll snooping around, how come nobody's noticed?' She also tried to implicate her in planting the gun."

"How'd she do that?"

Oops.

Cora's mind flip-flopped, realizing she didn't actually have an answer, at least not one she could give the chief. "By pretending the puzzle and the KenKen had been slipped under their motel room door," she improvised, tap dancing nimbly. "She knew when we found out Melvin's wife was staying at the motel, she'd be the most likely suspect."

"Yeah, yeah," Harper said, "but what about the gun?"

"She made up the puzzle and the KenKen to tell us where it was. Pretty clever on her part. The puzzle tells us to add up all the numbers. Of course, the numbers in the answer to a KenKen always add up to the same thing. If it wasn't the numbers in the answer, there was only one other thing it could be.

"Only we didn't think of it. Bambi can't believe it. What a bunch of dummies! She finally had to suggest it herself. 'Hey, maybe it's the numbers in the *problem*.' "

"You didn't notice that?"

"It's worse than that, Chief. I added 'em up and got ninety-three. It was Bambi who pointed out, 'No, that's wrong. It's really a hundred and six.' "

"So why did she plant the gun in the Pricherts' mailbox? Those people had nothing to do with anything. What did she hope to accomplish by that?"

"You got me there, Chief. That sure is strange. If she's clammed up, I guess we'll never know."

"Yeah." Chief Harper cocked his head. "As I recall, her theory was one oh six referred to the motel unit next to theirs. You and Sherry checked it out before you went to the mailbox."

"Some theories don't check out, Chief."

"They do if a theory's not just a theory but something you already know. She sent you to the motel to get the gun. She was shocked when you didn't find it. Right there in the motel room next to theirs, where it would look like Melvin's wife planted it."

"You make a strong case, Chief. Too bad she's not talking."

"*You're* talking."

"I'm talking about the *crime.* I'm not talking about my actions. You want to start talking about *my* actions, we'll get Becky Baldwin in here. That's going to take time, the media's waiting, you gotta make a statement."

"The problem is you think you can play fast and loose with the law."

"I don't, actually. I play fast and loose with people who *violate* the law. It's a big difference."

"You obstructed a police investigation. You tampered with evidence."

"Prove it. Charge me. Take me on. You wanna see a media circus, how about the Bakerhaven police and the district attorney gang up on the Puzzle Lady for helping them catch a killer and solving two crimes."

Harper scowled. "If that's the way you wanna play it."

"Hey, I don't wanna play it at all," Cora said. "This is your party. I just tagged along for the ride. It's a real feather in your cap, Chief. Solving two murders, catching a killer, and exonerating an innocent man."

"But . . ."

"But what?"

"How do I explain it to the media?"

"You don't have to explain, Chief. You're a winner. Take a few bows, run a victory lap." Cora smiled, patted him on the cheek. "You'll do fine."

CHAPTER 57

Melvin signed for his valuables and was released from jail. He came out the front door of the police station to find Cora Felton waiting for him.

"You here to gloat?"

"Gloat? They're not going to hang you, Melvin. Why should I gloat?"

"So why are you here?"

"Where's your wife?"

"She went home."

"She gonna take you back?"

"Wives always take you back. If they can win you away from younger girlfriends, there's such a feeling of empowerment."

"Giving away trade secrets, Melvin?"

"I never had any secrets from you." He smiled. "Not that I didn't try. You always saw through everything."

"You remember that fondly?"

"Okay, you were a major pain in the ass. I had more trouble with you than with any other woman. You realize you're getting more alimony than any of my other wives ever got?"

"Wow, what a distinction."

"It's not that you had a better lawyer. You were smarter than your average mindless slut."

"You are such a sweet talker, Melvin."

"I mean it. Being married to you was fun. You know why? Because you weren't a doormat on the one hand, or a shrew on the other. You were an equal sparring partner, giving as good as you got. If you'd been a little more tolerant, we'd have had a good thing."

"I didn't sign on for an open marriage, Melvin."

"I know you didn't. Did I flaunt women? Did I throw them in your face? But you made it your business to ferret them out. You hunted for reasons not to like me."

"Right, right. It wasn't your fault for running around, it was my fault for noticing."

"See, you're too good with words. I can't even argue with you."

"When you take an indefensible position, it's hard to win."

"This isn't about winning or losing. Jeez, Cora, we had a good thing."

"Yes, we did. Too bad it wasn't enough."

He winced. "Ah, gee."

"Of all my husbands, you're the one I hated most." Cora smiled ruefully. "Because you're the one who had the most potential. You're the one who hurt me most. You're the one I most hated to lose."

"You did care. I knew you did."

"Easy, Melvin."

Melvin studied the look in her eyes, tried to read her expression. "I always wondered why you never married anyone after me."

"I tried. It didn't work out."

"Some things were meant to happen. I don't suppose you'd consider giving it another go?"

"You're married, Melvin."

"I'm always married. It didn't stop you before."

"I'm older now."

"But you've still got it. That insane, loopy lust for life that lets you kick over the conventions. How many laws did you have to break to get me out of jail?"

"That's neither here nor there."

"You did, didn't you? You manipulated everything, played fast and loose with the police. Would you have done that for just anyone?"

"Yes. I'm that kind of a girl."

"So, we're not meant to be."

"Sorry, Melvin."

"I've still got that motel room. How'd you like to come back with me for old times' sake."

"Yeah, sure. Next thing I know your shyster would be filing papers for reconciliation."

"I'll have him draw up a disclaimer. Any actions taken this afternoon are not to be construed as having any bearing on the alimony hearing or the matrimonial state."

Cora hesitated. Melvin did look awfully good. She had to remind herself what a bastard he was. How angry she'd be with herself every time she thought of it.

Even so.

The man had incredible charisma, unlike anyone she'd ever met. They'd been good times, however brief, before it all went to hell. It was hard to turn him down.

Cora smiled slightly.

Wistfully.

"Sorry, Melvin."

CHAPTER 58

Aaron and Sherry were having champagne when Cora got home. Aaron met her at the door, handed her a glass.

"Aaron! I don't drink."

"It's ginger ale. Come on, we're making a toast."

Cora followed Aaron into the kitchen, where Sherry was sitting at the table, a glass in her hand.

"Kids, this is very nice, but I've solved cases before, and you never made a big deal."

"This one's special," Aaron said.

"Why?"

"You solved it in spite of the distracting presence of your least favorite ex-husband. Tell me, does being a murder suspect make him any more sympathetic in the annals of ex-husbandom, like maybe rise him from fourth place to third?"

"Once a creep, always a creep," Cora said.

She tried to change the subject. "How come you're not at the paper pounding out the story?"

"Already filed it. I wanted to be home for you."

"It's no big deal."

"Yeah, it is," Aaron said. "Sherry?"

Sherry smiled. "We're having a baby."

Cora's mouth fell open. "You said you *weren't* having a baby!"

"No. We said when we're having a baby, *we'll* tell *you* we're having a baby. Well, guess what. We're having a baby. Cheers!"

Sherry lifted her glass.

"You shouldn't be drinking that," Cora said.

"It's ginger ale. You going to be that way with the baby, too? A possessive worrywart?" Sherry's eyes widened. "Oh, my God. I just realized. You're going to be a great-aunt."

"Great-aunt, hell," Cora said. "I'm going to be the *greatest* aunt."

ABOUT THE AUTHOR

Edgar, Shamus, and Lefty finalist **Parnell Hall** is the author of the Puzzle Lady crossword puzzle mysteries, the Stanley Hastings private eye novels, and the Steve Winslow courtroom dramas. An actor, screenwriter, and former private investigator, Parnell lives in New York City. Visit his Web site at www.parnellhall.com.

The employees of Thorndike Press hope you have enjoyed this Large Print book. All our Thorndike, Wheeler, and Kennebec Large Print titles are designed for easy reading, and all our books are made to last. Other Thorndike Press Large Print books are available at your library, through selected bookstores, or directly from us.

For information about titles, please call:
  (800) 223-1244

or visit our Web site at:
  http://gale.cengage.com/thorndike

To share your comments, please write:
  Publisher
  Thorndike Press
  295 Kennedy Memorial Drive
  Waterville, ME 04901